AF415309

Farmington River

Farmington River

Stephen Leon

Stephen Leon

ACKNOWLEDGEMENTS

I would like to thank the beta readers who helped me see Farmington River through from beginning to end. They are: Hailey D'Amico; Mary Ann Donnaruma; Beth Henriques; Nicole Robertson; and Laura Clark Stedman. Their critiques and insights helped me to shape the novel in both subtle and substantial ways. Also, their encouragement and enthusiasm for the project helped keep my creative fire burning.

DISCLAIMER

This is a work of fiction. Names, characters, places, and incidents are the product of the author's imagination or are used fictitiously. Certain locales in the book are based on real places, but otherwise, any resemblance to actual persons, living or dead, or events, or incidents is entirely coincidental.

Chapter 1

Ethel Walker School, Main Auditorium
Simsbury, Connecticut
September 1982

"Mutual understanding, trust, honesty, communication, and support."

Victoria Lavelle enunciated each word in turn as she pointed to them one by one on the projection screen with her long pointer.

"Mutual understanding, trust, honesty, communication, and support."

"Where do we find these five qualities?" Lavelle asked, her high-pitched voice straining to fill the room full of Ethel Walker School sophomores and juniors.

"You," she demanded, pointing to a girl in the front row who was trembling and wishing she had sat somewhere else. Lavelle's pointer was stretched out like a long claw, almost touching the collar of the nervous girl's white blouse.

"In the classroom?" offered the girl weakly.

At that, Lavelle, a 50-something woman in a tan pantsuit

with her graying brown hair tied up in a bun, walked over to the girl and demanded to know her name.

"Jody Belanger," she replied.

"Wrong, Jody Belanger, wrong, wrong."

Lavelle smacked her pointer on the back of an empty chair with each "wrong." Then she thought for a moment, her frown still fixed on Jody Belanger, who was still trembling.

"Well, OK," Lavelle corrected herself. "You *might* find these qualities in a classroom, but probably not all at once."

"In a *healthy relationship*," Lavelle shrieked. "Don't you remember why we're here? To talk about relationships, and how to have healthy ones. God forbid you should start having relationships with boys before you know the first thing about what they're supposed to be like."

Before she gave much thought to what she was getting herself into, Lavelle blurted out, "Has anyone in this room kissed a boy yet?"

The question was immediately met with a combination of gasps and giggles.

When the commotion died down, a chestnut-haired girl in the front row spoke up.

"Why do you ask?" said the girl. "We're old enough to kiss boys. And whether you find it acceptable or not, we're hard-wired to do so."

Lavelle took a deep breath and clomped over to the girl in her tan, 2-inch-heeled boots. "And just what is your name, Little Miss Hotlips?" she asked.

"Mallory Harding," the girl answered without batting an eye.

"Well, Miss Harding, I do hope you have considered the consequences of kissing boys without even having the faintest idea what their intentions are."

"Oh, I know the consequences. I get a little lightheaded. They get a little lightheaded. My heart starts to pound. So does theirs. It's all quite thrilling, for the moment it lasts. But sometimes they think the kiss gives them a green light to--"

"Errrkk," Lavelle blurted out, doing her best to sound like screeching brakes. "We can just stop that line of thinking right there."

Mallory looked around the first two rows at her best friends, assembled near her, and smiled a triumphant smile.

"But since Miss Harding has alluded to the ways in which young boys might pursue their most deviant biological impulses, maybe this is a good time to talk about unhealthy relationships, which are often marked by persistent, unwanted sexual advances. And we aren't just talking about physical or sexual abuse here. Some boys will try anything to have their way, which might include various forms of emotional abuse. And for impressionable young women such as yourselves, making your way through your teenage years and preparing for your college education, it's important to recognize the many signs of emotional--"

"Excuse me?" Mallory waved her hand back and forth.

"What is it now, Miss Harding? I'm trying to teach an important lesson here about unhealthy relationships and emotional abuse."

"I would just like to be clear on one thing, Miss Lavelle. I'm well aware--" Mallory stopped to turn around and survey the auditorium full of girls. "As I think most of us are—that sexual and emotional abuse are problems we all might face sooner or later. I'm sure a few of us already have. And I'm grateful to you for educating us on the warning signs to look for. But again, I would never automatically equate sex with abuse. Or kissing with abuse. Nor would I ever assume any given boy is a sexually deviant predator just because of his biological desires. Nor would I consider it abuse when an overheated boy is just trying to see what he can get away with." Here, Mallory smiled, and looked around at her friends. "As long as he stops when I say so."

"Well," Lavelle said with an aggravated sigh. "Aren't we the confident free thinker. I'm surprised you're here and not being homeschooled."

Again, Mallory smiled triumphantly, as her friends looked on with awe.

"Sometimes I wish," Lavelle muttered to herself, but just loudly enough to be heard by the girls, "that we could just go back to good old Victorian virtues."

"Victorians had sex," piped up a soft voice from the second row.

"Wait a minute, who said that?"

A blonde-haired girl stood up and raised her hand.

"And your name is?"

"Catherine St. John, Ma'am."

"Miss St. John," Lavelle said, "Of course Victorians had sex —in marriage. That's how they propagated the English race."

"Unmarried Victorians had sex too."

"Speak up, Miss St. John. I can barely hear you. If you think you have something important to say, don't be so shy."

Cathy cleared her throat and coaxed her volume up a notch. "Unwed Victorians had sex too—assuming you believe the writers who described the era."

"OK, Miss Nineteenth Century Know-It-All. Name me one novel of the Victorian period in which unmarried characters had sex."

"Oh, dear, where to start?" said Cathy. "Maybe *Phineas Finn*? Granted, it's hard to tell sometimes, because they had to write the sex scenes in code."

Victoria Lavelle was not amused that she had been outwitted by a high school junior, and she momentarily lost sight of what she was supposed to be talking about as she reached desperately for a comeback. "Heathcliff and Catherine were the most celebrated Victorian couple of all time," she said, "and they never had sex."

"Subject to debate," muttered Cathy, sitting back down.

"OK, time to get back to the lesson," bellowed Victoria Lavelle, fumbling to replace the sheet on the overhead projector with a new set of words, which she enunciated while wielding her pointer like a sword. "Insults. Humiliation. Degradation. Manipulation. Intimidation. And worse: forced isolation, coercion, or use of fear or guilt to control or belittle."

"What am I talking about here?"

A brunette in the front row stood up.

"Name first, please," barked Lavelle.

"Maggie Duchesne."

"And your answer?"

"What is 'emotional abuse'?" Maggie said, smiling.

Lavelle, not getting the joke, frowned. "You're asking me?"

"No," corrected Maggie, "I'm answering you. That's my answer."

Lavelle, still confused, said, "Just 'emotional abuse' will do, thank you."

Maggie's best friend, seated next to her, did get the joke and was now doubled over, fighting off a severe case of the giggles.

"And you, young lady, if you are not too incapacitated to answer, would you mind telling me your name, and what exactly you find so funny?"

"Annie," the girl said as she stood up and tried to suck in another burst of giggles. "Annie Green. I just thought it was funny--" Here she stopped, exhaled, and tried to compose herself.

"You thought what was funny?" sputtered Lavelle, clearly becoming more impatient by the second.

As the giggles finally began to subside, Annie said, "You know, the way she gave her answer. In the form of a question. Like on that show--"

"That's enough nonsense for one day, Miss Green. Now, somebody choose from the first five words on this list, and let's talk about how an emotional abuser might use it against you. Volunteers? We still have a lot to get through. We haven't even talked about stalking yet. Or the differences between lust, infatuation, and love. She glanced at her watch. Again, volunteers?"

At some point, the Ethel Walker headmistress, Reisa Maitlin, had stepped quietly into the auditorium and was now seated in the back row. One by one, the girls noticed she was there, and realized it was time to get serious and help poor flustered Miss Lavelle get through her presentation.

Several hands shot up.

Miss Lavelle pointed to a young woman in the second row.

"Humiliation," she blurted out.

"Humiliation for 200," Maggie whispered to Annie, who shot Maggie an elbow to keep her from making her laugh again.

"Names *first*," screeched Miss Lavelle.

"Oh, I'm sorry. Melissa Clark. I'm choosing humiliation."

"And what might an emotionally abusive boy do to humiliate you?"

"Well, let's see," said Melissa. "You mean like if he didn't get his way with you? Like if you're making out, and he tries to feel you up under your shirt, and you don't let him get close enough to touch your boobs?"

Lavelle gasped. "Miss Clark," she said sternly, furrowing her brow as she spoke, "You don't have to be so graphic about it. But OK, so a boy tries to get fresh with you and you spurn him, what might he do to retaliate?"

"I think she's a time traveler from the 19th century," Maggie whispered to Annie.

"And she hasn't gotten laid in either century," Annie whispered back.

A girl on the other side of the auditorium raised her hand.

Lavelle whipped her pointer around and jabbed it in her direction. "Now don't for--"

"Lisa McInerney," the girl interrupted. "I have heard of boys who lie and tell their friends you're easy. But I really haven't seen much of that, not with our friends at Avon, anyway."

Another voice piped up. "Or they'll tell them--"

"Tut, tut, tut," Miss Lavelle scolded the girl who had spoken up, smacking her pointer three times on the empty chair next to her.

"Oh, sorry, I'm Beth Hoffman. I once heard of a boy who told his friends he did get under a certain girl's shirt and couldn't find any boobs."

"Couldn't have been talking about Maggie," snickered Annie, who got an elbow for her trouble.

Miss Lavelle looked like she was going to faint.

Mallory Harding and Reisa Maitlin stood up at the same moment, both entering emergency rescue mode. As Reisa stepped down the aisle, Mallory spoke.

"Miss Lavelle, if I may. Mallory Harding again. As I said before, we really do appreciate your teaching us how to be on the lookout for sexual and emotional abuse. I think some of the answers you're getting today reflect the fact that most of us are part of a tight-knit community of Walker's girls and our many friends at Avon Old Farms. We have spent a lot of our free time getting to know those boys, and they really are a great group. And they know their manners, for the most part. They're still teenage boys, but you can't hold that against them."

Annie Green covered her mouth to avoid an audible re-action to Mallory's unintended double entendre.

"And we are running out of time, said Maitlin, now standing in the center aisle about three rows back. "I'd like to quickly cover stalking, and then the difference between love, infatuation, and lust."

At this point, the flustered Lavelle was happy to cede the remainder of the presentation to the headmistress.

"You're all still young, so if you have experienced stalking already, it was probably by an older man who has psychological issues and is sexually attracted to young girls. If you ever experience anything like that here, with faculty or anyone else, you can come straight to me with it."

"As you get older, and you have had more time to develop relationships with boys and men, the danger comes from men who feel more emotionally attached than you do, and can't seem to let that go, and don't take rejection well. So they continue to pester you with phone calls, letters, showing up at places you go, and so on, even crying and pleading with you that they can't live without you. Well, they *can* live without you, and they will have to—that may be where a restraining order comes in."

Maitlin looked at her watch. "Not much time. Can someone--"

Lisa McInerney's hand came up. "Miss Maitlin, does it have to be a boy or a man? I mean, a girl could stalk another girl, right?"

"You mean like another girl who is sexually or romantically attracted to you?"

"Yes, a romantic attraction ... or maybe not even that," McInerney said. "What about someone who wants so desperately to be your best friend, and maybe you don't want to be that, but they won't take no for an answer?"

"Oh, I see," said Maitlin. "Yes, I could see that happening."

"OK, now, can someone explain the difference between love, infatuation, and lust?"

Mallory Harding stood up again.

"I'll do infatuation first. Infatuation is like a major crush, or even an obsession. You're not in a relationship, but you can't stop thinking of the person."

"That works," said Maitlin. Lavelle, apparently recovered, now stood next to her.

"And love?" asked Lavelle.

"Love," began Mallory, "is when you and another person form a deep emotional connection with each other. You feel intense affection for each other. You feel like you would do anything for each other. And you take tremendous pleasure--"

As she rolled the word "pleasure" over her tongue, Mallory could see the frown forming on Miss Lavelle's lips, and decided to just have fun with her.

"Pleasure ... pleasure ... in just being with them all the time. Talking. Listening. Holding their hand. Walking through the park arm-in-arm. Laughing at each other's jokes."

"Finishing each other's sentences," interjected Annie Green.

"Eating off each other's plates," added Maggie.

Reisa Maitlin chuckled along with most of the rest of the room.

"Now lust," began Mallory, "is when all you can think of is--"

Errrkk," Lavelle cut her off again with her screeching-brakes imitation. "That will do for today. Thank you all for having me here. Good luck in your studies, and good luck in becoming respectable young ladies."

Reisa Maitlin watched Victoria Lavelle stuff her papers back into her briefcase and stroll stiffly to the exit door. "Next year," she thought, "I'll try something else."

Reisa turned back to her girls, who had begun to stand up and collect their books and shoulder bags. "Don't forget, all-campus tea at 4 today. Let's make this the best year ever."

"Yes, let's," said Mallory Harding, smiling as she and the rest of the girls made their way to the auditorium exits.

Chapter 2

Avon Old Farms School, Avon, Connecticut
May 1983

The headmaster of Avon Old Farms School wanted nothing to do with the disappearance of Mallory Harding. When posters began to appear on the Avon campus, he ordered them removed. He did not take calls from the media about the case; his assistant told reporters he had no comment because there was nothing to comment on. The missing girl attended another private school in another town, and no one knew why she disappeared, or where to. There was no body, no evidence that a crime had been committed. For all anyone knew, she might be taking an impromptu rich-kid vacation in New York City, or Europe, or Cancun.

George Dickleman, the headmaster, picked up the phone and frowned a nasty, exasperated frown, though no one was in his office to see it. "No, no, no," he said, pausing for emphasis with each successive "no." "I told you not to bother even asking me. I don't want these—"

A closed door separated George from his assistant, Kathy Martin, in the next office. She knew he didn't want the calls, but was pretty sure he'd take this one. "George," she cut in finally, "it's Simon Savard."

Simon, a friend and fellow Yale alum, was a senior editor at the *Hartford Courant*. George took a deep breath and composed himself. "Good afternoon, Simon," George began. "How are you? How can I help you this fine Thursday afternoon?"

"Oh, I just called to say hi," Simon deadpanned. "Wondering how you've been doing. ... Oh, and we're also looking for a body, on the off chance—"

"OK, this is all off the record," George said, a hint of irritation returning to his voice. "And what do you know about this? Do you have anything new? I'm not interested in having our reputation smeared because a Walker's girl is missing and no one has the faintest fucking idea why. And I really don't think I need to see any more of your cubs sniffing around our school looking for a body to come tumbling out of a supply closet."

"George, George, George," Simon intoned slowly, hoping to massage his emotions and get him to ease up a little. "Ah, George, I know you have a thicker skin than that. The local newshounds will sniff around anywhere that looks promising, until it doesn't anymore. No worries. The police have no concrete leads on your campus. If that changes, you'll be the first to get a call from me."

Simon paused, then continued: "Now, I know you and your deputies keep an eye on who's doing what with the Walker's and Porter's girls. And I'm sure you already know that the Harding girl had lots of friends at Avon. She dated at least two of them, and it's likely that she was still seeing Arpante at the time she went missing."

George stared out his window. He knew Tomas was going to come up; there would be no stopping that. While George puzzled over how to respond, Simon changed the subject. "Hey, reunions are coming up in a few weeks. You coming to New Haven? We should meet for pizza and talk about something more pleasant than teenage girls meeting untimely deaths—"

"I know about Tomas Arpante," George finally snapped back. "Day student. The cops and reporters can find him at his home if they need to talk to him. Who's the other one?"

"The other one who dated Mallory Harding?"

"Yeah. I wasn't aware of another one."

"Hank Shahinian. Dated briefly back in the fall, as best anyone can tell. But the police so far have not named him as a person of interest."

"And Arpante?"

"Oh, I think they'll name him. But this is only a few days old. Last confirmed sightings of the Harding girl were Sunday late morning at Walker's. Now it's Thursday. And the parents in New Jersey just confirmed yesterday that she has not been there and has not contacted them."

George drew a heavy sigh, signaling his frustration with the unwanted drama, especially coming this close to the end of the school year. "Well, it seems to me that the investigations right now should be focused on the Ethel Walker School, where the girl lived. Have the police sent search teams to comb the area around that campus?"

"They've been over there, of course," Simon replied. "Listen, I'll let you go, George, but if you hear anything, you know where to find me."

"Thanks for the call, Simon. And if your reporters are going to be trespassing on my campus again, I'll be expecting that warning you promised!"

George hung up the phone and gazed out from his second-story office at the campus below. Dozens of teenagers filed by in their khakis and ties, along with a handful of faculty. The young male teachers—there were always several new ones, most of whom would stay a year or two, living in small apartments at the ends of dormitory halls, before leaving Avon to head off into a different life—looked almost indistinguishable from the fully grown junior and senior boys. The older teachers, the ones who gradually had come to terms with the possibility that long-term prep-school life suited them, slowly but surely, year by year, would grow into older, often more eccentric caricatures of their younger selves. If they stayed for the long haul, or got married and settled in with a spouse, or arrived at Avon as a teaching couple, they would be given a nicer apartment or even a small house on or near the main campus. And if they were peculiar old bachelors like Joe Kraft, they might fill that house over time with enough nautical knickknacks to make them feel like they were somewhere they'd rather be, and to make students who dropped by for extra math help feel like they had wandered into a maritime museum.

George looked at his watch. It was not quite two o'clock, and his afternoon was free until a department heads meeting and dinner beginning at five. He walked over to his desk. Reaching into the bottom left drawer, he pulled out a book of writings by Thomas Paine.

George's wife, Judy, worked in the Avon administration as the chief accounts receivable officer. They had met at a Yale party when he was a senior and she was attending a nearby community college. George had played football and baseball at Yale; that and his Ivy degree helped him land a series of prep school teaching jobs. Judy, now his young wife, followed along wherever he went, and they raised a son and a daughter. The children were now in their 20s; daughter Sally worked at a New York ad agency, while son Tom had returned to the roost to teach history at Avon. Now in his early 50s, George had aged well, while Judy's increasing boredom with her life seemed to manifest itself in the lines on her face and the puffing out of her once-attractive figure.

With the blur of early marriage, frequent moves, and rearing children now behind them, George and Judy conducted their marriage as a practical contract not to be disturbed by any behind-the-scenes drama—whether external (the missing Walker's girl) or internal (the chill that had descended on their bedroom). Judy Dickleman generally stayed out of George's office unless she was looking for him; she was not one to rummage through his desk drawers, let alone browse a Thomas Paine book. So his secrets were safe there.

He flipped through the pages, quickly finding and extracting the post-it note he was looking for. Scrawled upon it were the name "Caroline" and a local phone number. Two days earlier, he had been down on Route 44 meeting Caroline

Hartsburg for coffee to discuss the application of her son, Greg, to transfer from Simsbury High School and attend Avon Old Farms beginning in his junior year in the fall. Greg's academic record was middling by Avon standards, and it was not clear that he had much to offer Avon's highly rated sports programs.

Much clearer were the signals Caroline sent George to indicate that she would be open to making his admission decision on Greg easier—and that whatever that might mean, it would not be unpleasant for her. During the hour at the coffeehouse, she smiled at him frequently, which made her blue eyes sparkle. Her blouse was unbuttoned just low enough to attract his glances there, especially when she leaned in to validate his observations on people and life, clasping her hand on his wrist while laughing and saying "Tell me about it." She crossed and re-crossed her bare legs enough times to make sure he saw how long and toned they were. And once she noticed him noticing the shapely curve of her arch in her black patent-leather heels, she took to dangling one shoe to give him a better view.

As they got up to leave, she pressed a post-it note into his hand and said, "If there's anything else you'd like to know, don't be afraid to call."

In the parking lot, Caroline turned to him one more time to say, "I'm in real estate. Mostly flexible hours." She flashed a suggestive smile, and added, "Unlike my workaholic husband."

In his office, thinking about the hour in the coffeehouse, staring at Caroline's handwriting on the post-it note, and catching on it a whiff of her perfume, George felt a twitch in his groin. He reached for the rotary phone on his desk and began dialing.

Soon George was pulling into the rear parking lot of the off-campus apartment he kept under a fake name. He had instructed Caroline to time her arrival so that he would already be there, and to make sure his Saab was parked behind the building. She rang the bell, and he buzzed her in. He poured two glasses of red wine and handed one to her. "I enjoyed meeting you for coffee the other day," George began. "That was a very pleasant hour. It was interesting to hear all about your son, and about you."

"Yes, I had a nice time too," Caroline replied, smiling and raising her glass near her mouth as if about to take a sip. Before doing so, she paused and added, "As fun as that was, something tells me today is going to be even more fun."

They each took a sip of wine, but that was pretty much it for the drinking. Caroline set her glass down on a dresser, and George followed suit. Caroline kicked off her heels, took a step closer to George, and began running her fingers along the back of George's neck. Then she leaned in and gave him a long, soft kiss.

"I hope you're not in too much of a hurry," she cooed in between kisses to his neck. "I closed on a house this morning, and I'm good for the day."

"I have some time," he said, checking his watch and doing some quick math in his head. He began unbuttoning her blouse while she worked his belt buckle. Before long, she was falling back on the queen-sized bed, pulling him on top of her.

George forgot the outside world for an hour as he gave in to the charms of Caroline Hartsburg. After, as they lay on their backs, her legs crossed over his, they made small talk about the school and the small towns of central Connecticut. He checked his watch again. She checked to see if he might be up for another quickie before they parted ways for the day.

"Umm ... I see some potential here," she said, her eyes twinkling.

George laughed. "I hope you're not trying to kill me," he said. "You know, I'm not sure if Greg's acceptance has been processed yet, so you better watch how hard you work me."

With that, he laughed and climbed on top of her.

The pleasures of the afternoon had all but driven thoughts of the missing-persons investigation from George's mind. But little could he have known, as he and Caroline went at it a second time, that tip line at the *Hartford Courant* was ringing.

The reporter who answered took down a message, then walked it over to Simon Savard's office. The anonymous caller said she thought she saw Mallory Harding on Sunday near the Avon Old Farms campus, riding in an older-looking Buick Riviera, in the passenger seat, with Avon student Tomas Arpante behind the wheel.

Chapter 3

New York City
June 1983

It was the Friday after Memorial Day, so Young & Rubicam was on summer hours. For a few decades, most Manhattan ad agencies had been giving their employees Friday afternoons off between Memorial and Labor days; it was generally assumed that the ad execs who created the policy wanted to avoid rush-hour traffic on their way to the Hamptons. But in a magnanimous gesture that survived the years, they gave the afternoon off to the entire staff, most of whom were not in a social or financial position to spend their weekends among the high society at the eastern end of Long Island.

Sam Field could not afford a lot of travel, so most weekends he stayed put in Manhattan. But on June 3, 1983, he left his office on the 15th floor of Y&R at 12:30 with the duffel he had packed that morning in the small apartment he rented uptown. From 285 Madison Avenue, it was less than two blocks to Grand Central Station, where Sam bought a round-trip ticket to Hartford at the ticket window, and a bagel sandwich and Coke at Zaro's. He sat down on his duffel, leaning back against the wall, to eat his lunch and wait for the boarding call for his 2 o'clock train.

On the train, he tried to imagine what Avon Old Farms School would be like. He had seen pictures of the stone-and-oak, English Cotswold-style buildings and the smiling teenage boys, dressed either in the standard school-day uniform of khakis, coats and ties, or in Avon jerseys representing the many sports the school competed in. Sam expected to be coaching one of the soccer teams; George Dickleman had all but hired him when they met for an interview at the Yale Club of New York earlier that spring. This weekend's meeting, as Sam understood it, was merely a formality; sign a contract, finalize assignments, and receive an apartment key.

And Sam already had one foot out the door of Young & Rubicam. As an assistant media planner, he felt suffocated by the drudgery of crunching what to him were meaningless numbers, worsened by the abysmally low pay that left him frequently asking his father for a little more money so he could try to have a social life. When initially he had balked at the Y&R salary offer, his parents encouraged him to take the job anyway with assurances that if he worked hard, he'd move up the ladder and wouldn't always be this poor. He constantly reminded himself of that conversation to help overcome his guilt when he had to ask them, yet again, for money.

The Avon job offered exactly the same annual salary—plus room and board, and a chance to spend part of the day outdoors. To Sam, that seemed like a welcome escape from the crushing pace of the city. In their Yale Club meeting, Dickleman sensed that Sam felt that way, and used Avon's bucolic setting as a selling point. The headmaster saw in Sam what he always looked for in his young recruits: an Ivy League degree (the number of these among the faculty was highlighted in the literature provided to the parents of potential applicants), and a demonstrated facility for athletics. Two years of varsity soccer at Princeton convinced George that Sam could step into the role of head JV soccer coach immediately; his winter and spring coaching assignments could be worked out later.

As the train turned north toward Hartford, Sam began to wonder what kind of a social life, if any, was in store for him. On the romance side of the equation, he had already decided it couldn't be any worse than his experience in Manhattan. All of those beautiful New York women prancing around the city in their fashionable clothes had not brought him any meaningful companionship. He could count his brushes with romantic intrigue on one hand: a bad date with a woman from a media-buying company who had sounded funny and interesting on their many work calls, then didn't have much to talk about in person. An hour having a drink in the apartment of an Austrian woman who admitted she wasn't sure why she had invited him up, then took off her shirt, then promptly told him to get out. A hookup with a sexually aggressive woman visiting from Iowa that left him sore, sleepless, and unable to make it to work.

Only when Katie visited for a weekend did he truly enjoy female company: pleasant walks, conversations over inexpensive meals at ethnic restaurants, and warm, cozy lovemaking like they always shared when they managed to get together. Sometimes he thought they should see each other more often, but he worried that if they tried to do that, they would end up in the same place all over again: bickering over small things and feeling increasingly unsure they were ready to commit.

At Hartford's Union Station, Sam was met by a young history teacher named Tim Wright, who drove him to Avon Old Farms, about 25 minutes away. As the bustle of the city and Interstate 84 gave way to the country roads and pastoral vistas around Farmington, Tim gave Sam a quick lesson on the rhythms of the school, which rules you could bend, and so on. Young bachelor teachers, Tim noted, were in many ways treated like the students by upper faculty and staff. Tim promised to give him more pointers that evening when he and another teacher who hadn't left for the summer would meet for beers.

At 5:30 pm, Sam and another young recruit, Joe Grisman, met with several male faculty members and the dean of faculty. A catered supper was served in a wood-paneled conference room of the main administration building, as the men gave Sam and Joe an outline of life as an Avon "master." Each weekday begins with all students and faculty gathering for "morning meeting." Then classes, lunch in the refectory, more classes, afternoon sports, dinner in the refectory, and evening study hall.

Henry Hitchcock, the dean, leaned in toward Sam and Joe, the overhead light glancing off his shiny bald head, to emphasize the importance of lunch and dinner. While breakfast is served cafeteria style with students sitting where they please, lunch and dinner are more formal. Students and teachers alike dress in jackets and ties. Students sit in assigned seats on either side of long wooden tables with a master at each end. Meals are served family style, with everyone following proper manners as they pass the plates and bowls of food. Students must be excused by a master before they can leave.

Henry spoke deliberately in a deep, quavering baritone; that, his age ("not a day over 80, Sam and Joe would joke), and the fact that he never cracked a smile lent gravitas to everything he said.

"The most important thing is that the masters are at each end of the table, guiding them, making sure they mind their manners, giving them an adult role model that is not their parents. And you talk to them—about their days, about their goals, or most anything else they ask you to talk to them about. They are learning to have adult conversations in a way that is not the same as what they get at home. This helps give them the confidence to go forth take their place among their elders and peers in the college classroom, in the professional locker room, in the corporate boardroom."

At the end of the meeting, Henry asked the recruits to meet with him in his office. There, Henry handed Sam and Joe manila envelopes. "Take the time you need to go over this," he said, "but ideally, I'd like to have it back by tomorrow noon." Inside each envelope was a one-year contract.

Later that night, Sam, Joe, Tim, and Kevin Doolan, a math teacher and varsity football coach, sat in a pub on Route 44 in Avon, where suburban sprawl was steadily advancing from West Hartford. Several new chain restaurants had sprung up on 44, but Tim was partial to a locally owned diner that served a $1.99 breakfast of two eggs, toast, home fries and coffee. He didn't care that you could get breakfast for free in the refectory; slipping down to Fred's during his free morning period was his way of breaking out of the sometimes-stifling insularity of the campus. And the locally owned pubs had more personality than the chain restaurant-bars that had moved in.

At two and four years, respectively, Tim and Kevin were veterans of the young bachelors' club, and knew their way around the personality quirks and, in some cases, secret lives of the older faculty. The headmaster, George, didn't sleep with his wife, but was adept at bedding students' mothers. "There are certain boys whose misdemeanors you don't report to the administration—I'll give you a list," said Kevin with a dry, deadpan look Sam would get used to.

Joe Kraft, a math teacher in his 60s, was closeted, frustrated, and impatient to retire to the Maine seacoast, but pleasant on the surface. Then there was Juan Ortega, the Cuban-born math teacher and head varsity soccer coach. "He's a hoot," said Tim. "You'll get to know him pretty quickly. Sam, I understand you're going to be the J.V. coach."

"If you're lucky," Tim added, "Juan will tell you about the sex lives of the faculty."

"If you're lucky?" Kevin asked in mock surprise, the corners of his mouth turning upward has he glanced at Tim. Looking back at Sam and Joe, the mischievous smile still on his face: "If you're lucky, he won't tell you in such excruciating detail you'll wish he had never brought it up."

Frank and Merriam Rodriguez were another Cuban couple, both of whom taught Spanish; Frank was taking a sabbatical for the coming year. "She can't wait to be rid of him for a year," Kevin chuckled. "Wait till Juan tells you about their sex life. I can't do it justice; I can't smack my hands together that hard."

"Wait a minute," Joe said, looking a little concerned. "Does he beat her?"

Kevin laughed. "No, no, nothing like that. But Frank falls asleep in front of the TV every night by nine o'clock. Then at 5 in the morning he wakes up raging to go, if you know what I mean. She's still asleep, and all of a sudden he's on top of her ... well, imagine what Juan is trying to imitate smacking his hands together. You should let him tell you."

"How does Juan know?" asked Joe.

Kevin looked sideways at the young teacher and smiled a knowing smile. "Let's just say that Meriam talks to Juan more than she talks to her own husband."

Sam excused himself to use the restroom; on his way back to the table, he suddenly had a sensation that a woman in the bar was watching him. He was in a long hallway that opened up to tables ahead of him, with a long bar and more tables on his right. He scanned the crowd, but no one looked back; besides, he could have sworn the watching eyes were coming from his left. He turned to the wall, and then spun slowly around in place again, searching for the woman he felt certain was gazing at him.

He looked out into the noisy bar to listen for a tell-tale voice, but the conversations, what he could make of them as the voices droned and tumbled over each other, sounded dull and inconsequential.

"Never mind all of them."

The sudden, simple line came from a voice soft enough to be a whisper, yet it stood out from the others somehow. And it didn't seem to come from the tables, or the bar, or the long hallway to the restrooms. If anything, it seemed to come from inside his own head.

Slowly, Sam turned to the wall again, and there she was.

In an instant, Sam was mesmerized by the face on the wall in front of him. A young woman, probably in her late teens, looking over her right shoulder at the camera, her long, chestnut-brown hair tumbling over a red sweater, her lips parted in a slight smile, her deep-set brown eyes locked in a penetrating gaze that seemed to radiate out from the poster. Sam shivered as he took in the mysterious girl and pondered what magnetic force had somehow drawn him to look at her.

If the poster was alluring, its message was bleak. Mallory Harding, 17, Ethel Walker School student, missing since May 8. A number to call with tips, or any other information, however seemingly insignificant, that might be relevant.

Back at the table, Sam mentioned it to the others. Tim and Kevin looked at each other, then Kevin spoke.

"Yeah, it's tough. Missing without a trace. There was a Simsbury police detective snooping around the Avon campus a couple of weeks ago, trying to find anyone who might know something."

"George won't let them put up posters," added Tim. "Thinks it somehow makes the school look bad, and as far as anyone knows, there's no connection to Avon. She was last seen at Walker's."

"You're forgetting one thing," said Kevin. "Tomas Arpante."

"Yeah, she supposedly was dating one of our day students," said Tim.

"More than supposedly—that's what my kids tell me," Kevin said. Sam would soon learn that Kevin, one of the most popular teachers on campus, had a network of boys who hung around with him, and who supplied him with information, whether they realized it or not.

"Kevin's club," Tim laughed. "The eyes and ears of Avon."

"The detective took him in for questioning," Kevin continued. "Apparently he spent that Sunday afternoon with her, driving around, then drove her back to Walker's, then drove back home here in Avon. The detective must have thought he was convincing—or at least, the police seem to have lost interest in him for now. They had search teams scouring the Walker's campus and surrounding areas for a few days. That's all I know. George just wants the whole thing to blow over and leave the Avon campus alone. And he seems to be getting his wish."

"What do you guys think happened?" asked Joe.

Again, Kevin and Tim looked at each other, then back at Sam and Joe.

"I don't know," Kevin said finally. "I have no theory. I'm a teacher, not a detective."

"What about your kids? asked Sam.

"They don't know," Kevin said. "And even if they did offer a theory, you'd have to take it with a grain of salt. They know stuff sometimes—other times they just make stuff up. They're teenage wiseasses."

"Poor girl." Kevin shook his head. "Four weeks, gone without a trace, and the case is getting colder by the minute."

An hour later, as they all headed for the door, Sam said, "Gotta pee again. Catch up to you in a sec."

But Sam didn't have to pee. What he had to do was take one long last look at the picture of Mallory Harding.

Chapter 4

Simsbury, Connecticut
June 1983

Jackie Spellmeyer reduced the burner to medium-low to allow her saute pan to cool until it was safe to sprinkle in some minced garlic. She shook the pan vigorously a few times, then added in a cup of chicken stock and brought it to a boil while scraping up the browned pieces of chicken still stuck to the pan. She allowed the stock to reduce for a few minutes, then added some red wine, balsamic vinegar, and soy sauce. Finally, she returned the chicken and vegetables she had previously stir-fried to the increasingly aromatic mix, allowing every-thing to simmer while she prepared the rice. She was having fun spending more time in the kitchen again. Both Jackie and her husband liked to cook, but when both had been working, they didn't have much time for it, and ordered out a lot.

"Smells amazing, honey," boomed Jerry Spellmeyer from the living room of their home in Simsbury, where he was scowling at the day's stock-market numbers on the evening news. "Where have you been all my life?"

At 62, Jacqueline Spellmeyer had recently taken early

retirement from the West Hartford Police, where she had been a highly respected detective for more than 20 years. Now she had more free time to indulge other interests, like cooking, gardening, golfing, and furniture restoration. She also was happy to spend a little more time with her husband, although he still worked full-time at a brokerage firm in Simsbury.

"Almost ready to plate up, dear," she called out. A collie bounded into the dining room, then obeyed Jackie's command to "sit." Gradually, he would inch closer to the table. Jerry walked in holding the day's *Courant* in front of his face.

"What's new out there in the world?" Jackie asked her husband. "I spent most of the day golfing and gardening. So nice to be blissfully unaware of the news."

"Let's see. ... You know that section of I-95 that collapsed last week? Now they're saying the whole bridge may be unsafe. Gee, what was your first clue? ... The Bloomingdale mistress was murdered. ... Oh, here we go, excitement for the day. The Whalers have hired a new head coach. Poor guy. I'd rather dig ditches than coach that hopeless team."

"Still no leads on the whereabouts of the missing Walker's girl. There's a story today by Simon Savard—"

"Sounds like a hockey name," Jackie interjected. "Maybe he should try out for the Whalers."

Jerry chuckled as they both sat down.

"Duke, back off, you'll get scraps later," laughed Jackie, as the collie now was resting his snout on her thigh. "I know Simon, of course. So he's snooping around on this case too."

"The police questioned the Avon boy she was seeing, Tomas Arpante," Jerry continued. "Brad Sullivan, a detective from the Simsbury PD. He's quoted in the story. Said the boy's story is straightforward and consistent. Sullivan also talked to some more people on the Walker's campus—groundskeepers, stable hands, and so on. Most of the students are gone for the summer. And no one knows a thing. The boy says he dropped her off, but apparently no one saw her after she left that morning."

"Hmmm ..." Jackie suddenly seemed lost in thought. "I know Sullivan. Nice guy—maybe too nice. Not exactly the sharpest tool in the shed. I wonder ... Did he ask where he dropped her off? What time? Did Tomas say he saw anyone he knew? Something's not right here."

"Uh-oh," said Jerry. "You're not thinking of going down this rabbit hole, are you?"

"Oh, no, of course not, dear. But I would like to take a look at the story."

Later that evening, the couple retired to their living room, where Jerry switched on the TV and found the Red Sox game. Jackie opened up the *Courant* and began reading the missing-girl story, her mouth periodically screwing into a frown. "It amazes me sometimes—"

She paused. "Sometimes what?" asked Jerry.

"Oh, I should give them the benefit of the doubt. Maybe it was Simon who left out a few details. But I do sometimes wonder if they know what to look for."

Jackie put down the paper and opened up the book she was reading, but couldn't concentrate for very long. Her mind wandered. *If he really dropped her off at the school, but no one says they saw her that night, where did she go? Was she abducted as soon as he drove away? Or does he have something to hide? Is he being protected? And what other leads have they chased down?*

By then, Jackie had decided that in the morning, she would place a call to Reisa Maitlin, her longtime friend and the head of Ethel Walker School.

Reisa and Jackie had become friends from working together on a couple of Simsbury town committees. And the Walker's head had invited Jackie to speak at the school on a few occasions. Reisa thought it was important to show her girls positive female role models from a variety of professions, from business to the arts. And she thought a successful, no-nonsense police detective was pretty darn cool. The girls thought so too—Jackie's talks always ended with spirited question-and-answer sessions.

Jackie pulled her Volkswagen Rabbit up to the front of Beaver Brook, the main academic and administrative building, where Reisa was waiting outside. "You can just park it here," she said. "School's out for the summer."

Indeed, the campus was serenely quiet apart from the sound of lawn mowers and an occasional human voice from the equestrian summer camp across the road. Reisa led Jackie to her office, where she poured each of them a cup of tea, and motioned to a pair of comfortable chairs to the side of Reisa's mahogany desk. They made catch-up chat for a few minutes, then Jackie set her cup down on a table, and said, "I know you're probably tired of this, but—"

"It's OK," Reisa smiled. "I know why you're here. Ever the detective, even in retirement!"

Jackie drew a deep breath and began. "I've been reading the accounts of this, and something just doesn't feel right. I can't put my finger on it."

"I'll say something doesn't feel right. And Mallory was—oh, excuse me, sometimes I can't help but be pessimistic about this. Mallory *is* such a bright, beautiful and vivacious girl. Lots of friends. The dream girl of all the Avon boys. Meanwhile, I've got angry parents, befuddled investigators, and a campus full of people who have basically zero clues to offer."

"Do you know if she had any enemies?" Jackie asked. "Any threats ever reported against her? Jealous ex-boyfriends?"

"No enemies or threats that I've ever known about. Or jealous ex-boyfriends. Just the current boyfriend, and she was with him that day, under apparently typical circumstances."

"How are her friends taking it? And the rest of the girls in general? If I were a teenage girl and someone went missing from campus, I'd be freaking out. Did the school offer counseling?"

"Yes, of course. A hotline people could call. A dedicated office we staffed with counselors from early morning till the end of evening study hall. I just don't know ..."

"Don't know what—if it helped?"

"I'm sure it helped the girls who used it. But only a handful did. It's funny, we're so geared here to handle the problems we expect: academic concerns, roommate problems, boyfriend problems, sexuality issues, and depression over any of those things or over nothing at all. Teenage girls are Petri dishes of raw emotion. But something like this ... You don't think this will happen, and you hope it won't happen, but then you end up not thinking about it much at all. Then it does happen, and at first you hope it will resolve itself quickly: *Hey, guess who's back? She had a fight with her boyfriend and took a couple days off to spend with her parents.* But then it doesn't. And the shock sets in."

"Speaking of her boyfriend, what do you make of Tomas?"

Reisa sighed and thought for a moment, then answered, measuring her words carefully.

"You know, I met him once or twice. Seemed like a nice kid. Day student, maybe working-class, father works in a restaurant, mom a part-time receptionist. If he had any trouble fitting in at Avon, I'm sure the sports helped. He's good at everything. I hear he's getting a baseball scholarship to UConn. Maybe he got a little cocky from his success on the field—I see that, but if there's any issue with how he treats women, I don't know anything about it."

"It's the story he gave that gives me pause," said Jackie. "By now everyone knows that he picked her up in his car and they spent the afternoon together. He says he dropped her off here around 5:30. Everyone remembers seeing her in the morning, but no one remembers seeing her in the evening. Wasn't she supposed to sign back in to campus? What about her roommate?"

"The boarding students are all supposed to sign out when they leave campus and sign back in when they return. On weekends, a faculty dorm resident on duty is supposed to oversee this. Students are to be back by 7 unless they have prior permission. There is some confusion as to whether the faculty member, Miss Higgins, noticed a problem with the sign-in or sign-out. By around 10 o'clock, Mallory's roommate, Suzanne Fiorini, became worried enough to let Miss Higgins know she still hadn't returned. One of them called it in to an administrator on duty. But I didn't find out until the next day."

"One of the problems," Reisa said, sighing again, "is that it takes a day to two days for it to sink in that she's missing without a logical explanation. On Sunday night, none of the girls are thinking too much about it at first—girls have been known to be late, especially if they have boyfriends. When it starts to sink in the next day, it's still confusing, and everybody's still waiting for a logical explanation. So you begin to lose the immediacy of remembering what you saw, or didn't see, the night before."

"It would be different, "Reisa continued, "If something concrete happened here on or near the campus. A car crash, a fight, loud angry voices. A party at a nearby house. Even a trail of blood. Now you can ask people what they saw or heard. When nothing happened as far as anyone knows, there's no point in asking questions like, *Did you hear loud voices around 5:30 pm?* Or *Did you see a strange man speed away in an old Buick?*"

"Yeah, I get that," said Jackie. "It's hard to find out more about something when there isn't even a something to start from. From the standpoint of the detective, missing persons cases can seem like groping around in the dark until you get something to work with. Tomas could be that something, but the detective in charge seems to have moved on. What about

Mallory's close friends? Who are her closest friends? Have you spoken with them?"

"Well, yes, actually. I spoke with two of her best friends before they left for the summer—Annie Green and Maggie Duchesne. Again, they don't have a clear memory of that Sunday night. I did ask them how well they knew Tomas. Pretty well, it seems. It's funny, the schools are four miles apart, but you'd be surprised how close Walker's and Avon are in terms of how many friends they make across the two campuses. Sometimes it seems like they all go to the same school."

"Anyway," Reisa continued, "they like Tomas. And they don't see him as a violent person. In fact, they said he treated her very well. But ..."

"But what?"

Reisa leaned in, and spoke in more of a hushed voice, almost as if there were other people trying to listen in. "Well, I got a strong impression that they just don't believe his story about dropping her off here that night. That the real story may be more complicated, and that there may be something he's not telling. They just didn't say what."

Chapter 5

July 1983

When the flow charts first appeared on the large dry-erase board in Jackie Spellmeyer's home office, and her husband began to find lists on lined legal pads that Jackie had left on tables near where she had been sitting, he knew there was no stopping her. Not that he minded; her work had always given them plenty of new, interesting things to talk about.

On a Saturday morning in July, Jackie had a quick breakfast with Jerry before dressing in a light-gray jacket with matching slacks and a simple black top; just casual enough to look professional but approachable. Her leather briefcase contained only her C.V., a pen, and a couple of yellow legal pads. She got into her Rabbit and drove 2 hours and 45 minutes to a house in Summit, N.J., where Charles and Mackenzie Harding greeted them at the door.

The couple seemed reluctant at first to open up about Mallory, though they warmed up to Jackie as they listened to her talk about her experiences with missing persons cases, and fielded her questions about Mallory. Jackie cautioned that such cases often do not turn out well, though she had seen a number of pleasant surprises (and less pleasant ones, like young people whose disappearance was deliberate). Above all, Jackie said, she would report back concrete findings, and take care not to overstate leads that might give false hope.

Through her questioning, Jackie learned that Mallory was a free thinker, and since that was encouraged in the Harding household, she was not particularly rebellious; she had never run away or disappeared, and seemed emotionally stable; because she left for prep school in 9th grade, she had relatively few close friends in Summit, though the ones she did have seemed to admire and look up to her; and she adored her older brother Stuart, who was, with his parents' encouragement, entering his senior year at Brown on time. Mallory played piano and violin passably well, and ran track, but her No. 1 passion, which she was grateful to indulge at Walker's, was horses.

Toward the end of their lunch, Jackie apologized in advance before asking a question she always asked: In recent years, had there been any significant turbulence in the household—major disagreements with either of the children, financial problems, marital problems, anything like that?

Charles and Mackenzie looked at each other and shrugged their shoulders. "I'd say we're a pretty drama-free household," Mackenzie said, smiling.

Jackie smiled back; later, she would note that it was the first and only time in their conversation when the Hardings' answer struck an off tone.

Before leaving, Jackie offered to take their case as a private investigator for a small fee ("Don't worry, I'm well set up for retirement") plus expenses. A few days later, Charles Harding phoned Jackie to accept.

At about four-thirty on a Thursday afternoon, Jackie dialed the number she had for Mario and Anna Arpante. Anna answered the phone with the soft and halting tone of someone who has lately taken more calls than she ever would have expected or wanted to. She listened as Jackie identified herself as a private investigator and former West Hartford police detective, and made her pitch to speak with Tomas, either alone or with his parents present, just to clear up some information that seemed vague in the newspaper accounts.

Anna sighed heavily, then finally spoke. "This is exhausting, you know. And I thought it was over. The Simsbury police have already spoken with Tomas. And now you? Who do you work for again? My son is innocent. When do we get to have some peace?"

"I understand your frustration," Jackie replied in a steady, assuring tone. "I've been hired as a private detective by the girl's parents."

Jackie paused for a second to let Anna take in that she was, in fact, working in an official capacity.

"This by no means suggests that Tomas is responsible. I just like to be thorough, and I don't think the police have asked all the right questions yet. Tomas may well be innocent, but he also may have information that will help us find the girl."

After a pause, Anna said, "OK, I'll talk to Mario when he comes home tonight. I have your number."

"And what about Tomas? Can I speak with him?"

"I need to discuss this with Mario first. Tomas isn't here anyway. He has a game tonight."

"Oh," Jackie said, trying to sound more conversational than inquisitive. "Baseball? Does he play in a summer league?"

Anna was fooled by Jackie's façade of harmless curiosity, or she might not have let her pride take over and divulged so much information.

"He plays for the American Legion team in West Hartford. Tomas is a star player, you know. He was heavily recruited to play at UConn. His coaches consider him a major league prospect, and Legion is where the best high school graduates play in the summer."

"Thank you. And good luck to Tomas. I hope to hear from you soon."

Jackie hung up the phone and looked at her watch. Jerry would be home soon with the *Courant*.

When he walked in, she asked him, "Honey, does the *Courant* sports section cover American Legion baseball?"

"Hit and miss," he replied. "Are you looking for something in particular?"

"Game tonight."

"OK, give me a second."

Jackie didn't bother to try to find the information herself; she knew her husband would know exactly where to look.

Jerry, now seated on the couch, began flipping through the sports section. "OK, here we go. American Legion. Two games today. Simsbury at Meriden, Bristol at West Hartford. Does your boy play for Simsbury?"

"West Hartford. What time is the game?"

"Five-thirty. Conant High School. It's five-thirty now. You thinking of going? Maybe you can catch him after the game. They play seven innings, maybe two hours tops. I know where the school is. Do you?"

"Yeah, it's right between 84 and Rockledge Golf Club. I have golfed there. I'll find it. You want to get Chinese or something?"

"Sure. Or Japanese."

"You pick. You know what I like. I should be back by 7:45, 8 if he actually stops and talks to me."

"The kid is quite a prospect, I hear. Not surprised he's on a Legion team—that's where a lot of future major leaguers play. How much you want to bet he plays Cape Cod League next summer? We should go see him play there."

"I'd like to solve the case first."

Jackie had a passing interest in baseball; she was not a fanatical Red Sox fan like her husband. But watching Tomas Arpante gracefully handle his chances at third base, and smack two line-drive doubles into the gap, she could tell there was something special about him.

West Hartford won the game, and the players did their ritual congratulations and backslaps. Tomas packed up his equipment bag, took off his cleats and put on slides, and dangled keys as he walked toward the parking lot. But before he could get into his Buick Riviera, Jackie, who had waited to make sure other players were out of earshot, startled him by stepping in front of him.

"Mr. Arpante, I just wanted to congratulate you on

the game, and introduce myself. My name is Jacqueline Spellmeyer."

Tomas looked puzzled and mildly annoyed.

"I'll get straight to the point: I'm a private investigator. Not the police. I'm just on a fact-finding mission. I've been hired by Mallory's parents. I know this has been hard for you."

"Can we talk about this another time?" he said.

"Of course. Whenever is convenient for you, and wherever is comfortable. Again, I'm not accusing you of anything. Missing persons cases are tough, and I have very little to go on here. So one of the protocols is talking to everyone who knew her well and saw her before she disappeared."

Tomas stood about six feet tall with dark hair, a Mediterranean complexion and dark eyes. Jackie was conscious of, but not intimidated by, his rugged good looks. "OK," he said finally. "I'm going to be pretty busy this summer—a lot to do before I leave for college. I'll see what I can do to find a little time."

"I do appreciate it, Mr. Arpante," Jackie said, choosing her words carefully. "And again, I'm sorry for what you must be going through. I understand you were close."

Tomas looked at Jackie with a hint of curiosity, wondering what she was fishing for. "Yes," he said finally. "It has been a painful time. For all of us who knew her."

Jackie paused momentarily as she considered the subtle nuance of his answer, and thought better of pressing him for more. "Thank you," she said, handing him a business card. "I hope to hear from you. I'm sure anything you can tell me would be helpful."

She watched him climb into the Riviera, a pale beige 1973 model with rust around the wheel wells. "Hand-me-down car?" she smiled.

"Yeah, Dad gave it to me a couple of years ago."

The door closed behind him. As he drove away, Jackie made mental notes of a few things about the car she might want to remember later. An Avon Old Farms day-student parking sticker, a tattered Boston Red Sox bumper sticker, a few scratches and dents, mostly small and narrow, plus a slightly larger, round-ish one on the passenger-side door. There was nothing flashy about the car, and nothing dangling from the rear-view mirror that might hint at a personal interest or trait. The family probably had dropped collision from the insurance and had little interest in paying for body work. To Tomas, apparently, the Riviera was transportation, nothing more.

Back home, Jackie took a seat at the kitchen table while Jerry heated up her noodle soup and shrimp tempura.

"Well, did you see him play? Did you talk to him?"

Jackie seemed distracted. "Excellent player," she said finally.

"Is that all?"

"Not quite. I caught up to him in the parking lot. We had a brief conversation. I ..."

Jerry was always interested in his wife's first impressions of suspects and witnesses—especially as she was almost always right.

"Go ahead. You know your first read is my favorite part."

"Well, he hasn't really told me anything yet. And he

doesn't really want to. So he knows things he hasn't told me or the police detective or anyone else. And yet ..."

Jackie paused again.

"I'm still here!" Jerry laughed, although he knew Jackie would take a minute to sort out what she wanted to say before actually saying it.

"It's funny. I think he's tired of being questioned. And I think he feels bad about whatever happened to Mallory, though I also get the sense that emotionally, he has moved on. But he's not particularly nervous. He does not seem worried about being caught, which tells me that, more than likely, he has not committed a crime. So he may be as baffled as the rest of us. But there's still a big missing piece, and if he knows what it is, he's not telling."

Chapter 6

September 1983

On a warm, sunny Wednesday afternoon in early September, Juan Ortega sized up the scene in front of him, then boomed in his distinctive, gruff, Cuban-accented baritone, "You want to play varsity soccer for Avon Old Farms? You want to play varsity soccer for Avon Old Farms?"

All of the students who had chosen soccer for their required fall sport were gathered in a semi-circle around Ortega; behind him stood several teachers who would handle coaching duties for the J.V., thirds, and fourths squads.

Ortega paused for effect, then continued:

"You want to compete for the state prep-school championship? You want to beat Westminster? Be prepared to *work!*"

"Now, those of you already invited to play varsity this year, go stand over here." Sixteen players followed the order. "Hmm," continued Juan. "I may have a few more spaces. Is there anyone who played J.V. last year who thinks they deserve a chance at varsity?"

Seven arms shot up.

"OK, you better be good! You better be better than I think you are!"

At this, three boys slowly lowered their arms, then one raised his again.

"Come on," Juan said with a hearty chuckle. "Give yourself some credit. If you don't think you're good enough, then why should anyone pass to you? Come on over and show me what you can do. I can't keep all of you, but you are welcome to try out."

Juan then turned around, and pulling several roster sheets from his clipboard, handed them to the other coaches. "I split them up based on their age and whether they had played for Avon at any level the previous fall," he told them. "Nothing is set in stone yet. Take them to your field and start them on drills. As you get to know them, you can shuffle them around till they seem to be where they belong. We'll figure it out." Turning back to his varsity players, he barked, "and we'll win that state championship!"

Sam looked at the list in his hand, announced "I'm Coach Sam Field," and began calling out names of students to follow him to the J.V. field. His co-coach, Steve Morrow, stood beside him. On the somewhat awkward first day of practice, each coach assumed they would be the one in charge; Steve because he had been here a year and had coached thirds, and Sam because he had a soccer background and had been told by George he would be head coach.

"Joe Adams," Sam read from the list.

"Here," replied Joe. Sam waved him over to the field and

continued though his list. "Nicolas Arpante, Bart Bazeby, Tony Blake, Bill Brody, Dan Contini, Tommy Dolan—"

"He went up to varsity," Steve said with the self-assurance that came with the fact that he knew the kids already and Sam didn't.

"Mike Farmer—"

"He went with the varsity too."

Sam tried to hide his irritation as he continued. "Niels Fredricksen, Greg Hartsburg, Randy Holloway, Sam Honeycutt—"

"Varsity."

"James Longworth, Eugene Jackson, Mike Marder, Josh Markowitz, Dean McGrath, Freddie Nash, Bob Scott, Hank Shahinian, Rick Stringfellow--"

"Varsity."

"Graham Toomer, Miles Tucker, Ali Touran, Rob Westerveldt."

"Rob went with the varsity too."

"Well then, looks like that's everyone for now." Sam dug right into a passing drill, trying to assert control over the situation. "Four groups, five each, two lines facing each other, about 10 yards apart. One ball for each group of 10."

The boys, confused at first by Sam's directions, struggled to organize themselves. Steve wanted to say something but didn't.

"Come on," Sam barked. "This shouldn't be hard. "Five in a line facing another five, then the same thing several yards over. ... That's better, but more space. This line, take two steps to the right."

Sam stood at the front of one of the lines with a ball. "Pass the ball, inside of your foot, on the ground, squarely to the guy across from you, then follow your pass and head to the back of the other line. You," he said, pointing, "receive the pass and settle it at your feet with one touch, then pass back to the other line."

Sam demonstrated, taking extra care to make sure his pass was crisp and on target.

"Right foot first. Let's go."

The boys did the drill for 20 minutes or so, right foot then left, then Sam switched the instruction to one-touch, meaning they had to pass to the other line without settling the ball first. At first, this produced more errant passes that skittered to the side or landed in the wrong line. Sam glanced at Steve and said, "We'll get there."

They moved on to another drill, then another, and soon they were playing mini games of 2-v-2.

Sam and Steve discussed the players, and agreed to send Joe Adams down to thirds. Juan sent them back two players.

Sam pulled Hank Shahinian aside to offer a couple of pointers, and while he was distracted, Steve sent Bob Scott down to thirds. When Sam saw the young sophomore running off to the other field, he was miffed, but tried not to show it. He was starting to like Steve and wanted it to work out. "Oh, OK, I didn't watch him very much yet. Let's talk it over next time."

Sam made notes on the roster sheet on his clipboard as he watched the players run through drills. One name already had jumped out.

"Did Nick Arpante play with you on thirds last year?" Sam inquired.

"Yeah, pretty good player. Goes by 'Nico,' actually. Should do well on J.V. Can be a little hot-tempered at times."

Sam remembered the name Tomas Arpante as a possible person of interest in the case of Mallory Harding, the missing Walker's girl. He was pretty sure Tomas had graduated. But seeing the name reminded him of the photo of Mallory that had haunted him back in June.

"Did he have a brother who went here?"

"Yeah," Steve replied, "Tomas. Graduated last spring. Got a baseball scholarship to UConn. Why do you ask?"

"Oh, nothing," Sam said. "I just heard he was an exceptional baseball player."

"No slouch on varsity soccer, either," Steve added.

Sam whistled the end of the drills, and gave the team a water break while he jogged over to Coach Ortega to get an idea how much time they had for a scrimmage.

"Oh, I'll give it another half-hour," Juan said. "Just make sure they run gassers at the end."

"Gassers?"

"Wind sprints. To make sure they run out of gas and get plenty of sleep tonight. First day of classes tomorrow."

Sam and Steve split the boys into three teams of seven for half-field scrimmages with small goals. As he watched the boys play, Sam noticed how pleasant it felt to be outside on a gorgeous September afternoon. In Manhattan, he would have been couped up in his 15th-floor cubicle, no windows in sight, staring at charts of sales numbers, wondering why the hell he should care how many cans of Chef Boy-Ar-Dee were sold last month in the company's test markets.

When it was time, Sam blew his whistle and shouted out: "Line up along the line here. When I blow the whistle, jog to the halfway cone and sprint back. Then jog to three-quarters and sprint back. Then jog the full field and sprint back. We'll do that a couple of times. You get the idea."

As they ended the last sprint, Sam noticed two boys shoving each other. Then they started to swing their fists, as their teammates rushed in to pry them apart. One was junior Graham Toomer; the other was Nico Arpante.

"Whoa, what's going on here," Sam yelled, rushing in to help separate everyone.

Graham had a smirk on his face; Nico was visibly angry. "Tell him to shut the fuck up," Nico half screamed, half sobbed.

"What did he say?" asked Sam, holding Nico back by the shoulders.

"Ask him."

Steve Morrow was already escorting Graham away, speaking to him softly but earnestly.

As all four practices ended, the boys gathered up their gear, broke into small groups, and began the short walk through the trees and back to the main campus. A Chevy pulled up on the side of the road adjacent to the fields; it was Anna Arpante, waiting for her son.

Juan Ortega walked over to where Sam and Steve were standing. "So what was that little altercation about?"

Steve sighed. "Toomer said something ... unfortunate."

"That tells me you heard it," Juan said.

"Mostly. Something to the effect of, 'Did your brother tell you where he hid the body?'"

"Uh-oh, Jesus Christ, not good," growled Juan. "I'll have a word with the two of them."

"Is this going to be a problem all season?" Sam asked.

Juan turned to Sam with a look that assured he would take care of it. "No," he answered flatly. "That's why I'm going to have a talk with them. And if Graham can't play by my rules, he can run cross-country. I'll make sure he understands that."

Steve and Sam had both walked to practice from campus, but Juan had his car, and wanted a word with Sam. "I'm going to give Sam a ride back, Steve. See you tomorrow."

Steve understood that Sam was about to receive a dose of Juan's eccentric wisdom. He waved and trotted off.

Juan unlocked his Fiat Strada hatch and tossed his ball bag into the back. As they climbed into their seats, Juan said, "How'd it go today?"

"Um, fine, I guess."

"Steve will be fine. He's a good guy. He knows the players, but you'll know them soon enough. I can tell you know the game."

Juan continued. "Toomer's a wiseass. Make sure he knows you won't put up with that kind of crap. And watch Nico. He has a hot temper sometimes. But he's a good kid. His brother's a good kid. And I know their parents. Nice family. Hard-working. Originally from New Haven. I think his dad worked in the pizza business there before someone he knew opened a place in this area, and Mario got offered more money to cook up here."

"Any other questions or problems with the players, don't be afraid to ask."

Sam replied, "So far I don't know much about them, except for that incident today. Now, there is one boy I'm curious about—Hank Shahinian. Nice enough kid, I think, and seems athletic, but—"

"But doesn't show it?" Juan said knowingly.

"Something like that. He looks like he could be better than he was today. That's why I didn't send him down."

Juan sighed. "Work with him. You'll like him. Try to understand that he's not gung-ho on sports like the rest of them."

As they drove past the soccer and baseball fields toward Old Farms Road, Sam motioned to more soccer fields across the road. "Is all of this part of Avon Old Farms?"

"The town owns those fields. We can rent them when we have overflow. The youth program is based there. Fisher Meadows, nice park with a big pond and hiking trails. Busy sometimes, but not always. There are secluded areas down toward the Farmington River."

A wry smile crept across Juan's face, as it typically did whenever he got on his favorite subject.

"The kids go down there to park."

"Our kids?"

"Our kids, town kids, whatever. All you need is a car, a boy, and a girl, maybe some beer."

Juan turned and looked at Sam as he turned the Fiat onto

Old Farms Road. "If you drive by at the right hour, you can practically hear them fucking."

September 1983

Sam Field stood at the head of his European History class with one hand resting on his desk. A week and a half of teaching, and he was beginning to feel more relaxed in the role. He was aware of one annoying habit he couldn't seem to break, his tendency to pause and say "Anyway …" as he prepared to pivot to a new thought or subject. But his lesson plans were filling up the class time nicely. He smiled as he remembered a friend from Princeton who had taken a job teaching at St. Paul's School in Concord, New Hampshire, talking about his first week as a teacher, walking over to the blinds several times during class to open and close them, because he had run out of things to say.

"Okay, your homework for the rest of the week is, one, finish reading the chapter on the Renaissance, two, be ready for a pop quiz—"

"Mr. Field, what day is the pop quiz?" cut in Jeff Banks with his usual nonchalant disregard for classroom manners.

"It's a pop quiz," responded Sam. "As in 'pop.' Like it

pops up without warning. Could be Wednesday, could be Thursday, could be Friday—"

"Could be yesterday, in which case we all missed it and don't have to worry about it anymore," piped up Chet Hennessey, Banks' chief rival for class clown.

"Hennessey, you just go on living in your fantasy world. There will be a pop quiz this week. And you will be graded on it. And if you find out which day the quiz is, and you decide to skip class, that grade will be a big fat zero. Now ... where was I? Oh yeah, number three, pick out a significant figure from the Renaissance and write a 750-word report on that person, citing your sources."

"How about ZZ Top," asked Banks. "Do they count as Renaissance?"

"I don't know," replied Sam with a straight face. "Are they from the 16th century?"

"They're pretty old," replied Banks.

"And the chick on MTV said they're having a renaissance," chimed in Hennessey.

"Okay, Banks, I gave you the assignment. You know what to do."

"Okay? Are you saying it's okay to write about ZZ Top, Mr. Field?"

"Sure," replied Sam. "Assuming they recorded 'Tush' in Italy in the 16th century."

Banks smiled weakly. "How do you know 'Tush,' Sir?"

"I'm 24, not 64."

Sam stepped out into the sunshine and walked across the quad to his apartment, which he dropped off his text and notebooks. Reemerging, he spied Juan Ortega and Kevin Doolan chatting in the center of the quad.

"There he is, the new guy," announced Kevin. "How's it working out for you so far? I hear the kids like you as coach."

Sam expressed surprise that Kevin had heard anything.

"Oh, he's got his little gang of informants," laughed Juan. "Look over there, they're starting to gather by his door."

"Hey, they keep my dog company," said Kevin.

"You guys heading over to lunch?" Sam asked.

Just then, George Dickleman hurried by, looking at his watch.

"Must have an important appointment," snickered Juan.

Sam cocked his head, trying to read Juan's sarcasm.

"I told you about George, didn't I?" said Kevin. "And his little black book of hot mothers? And the secret apartment he keeps that no one else knows about, except that we know it, and he doesn't know we know it?"

"Oh, and Kevin, I think he's fucking a new one now. That's probably who he's going to see. She got her kid in as a transfer from Simsbury High. He moved on her quickly."

"Oh jeez, Sam, did I ever give you the list?" asked Kevin.

"The list?"

"The boys whose misdemeanors are not to be reported under any circumstances."

"Sam," Juan said, "If you try to report one of these kids, and George is fucking his mother, he'll punish you worse than the kid. Kevin, you can add Greg Hartsburg to the list."

"There was a guy about your age here last year, Tom LaFlore, taught your European history sections, said Kevin.

"Poor guy, slight build, he caught Hank Shahinian drinking or some such thing. Tom thought he was supposed to report it. George thought he might like to keep doing Hank's mom when she popped in every few weeks from Worcester. So he finds Tommy, and tells him, 'Next time you catch a kid breaking the rules, take care of it yourself. Grab him by the lapels and slam him up against the wall.' And with that, George grabbed Tommy by his lapels and slammed him up against the wall. 'See? Like this.' "

Seated at the end of a long wooden table in the refectory, Sam and the students seated on either side of him executed the now-familiar ritual of passing plates and bowls of food around. There was chicken and pasta, salad and rolls, along with pitchers of water and milk. Sam chatted with the boys closest to him; his friend, Joe Grisman, seated at the other end, did likewise. They talked about their classes, sports, weekend plans, nothing too deep or personal. As the boys got to know Sam, if they wanted to talk about something more serious, they'd catch him in the quad or knock on his apartment door.

As Sam left the refectory, he passed by Kevin Doolan's apartment, where Kevin was now holding court with several boys before the start of afternoon classes. Have you guys met Mr. Field?" Kevin asked before introducing them. "And here's Max," he added, as a bulldog mix ambled over to give Sam a sniff.

They talked a few minutes longer, before Kevin announced it was time for class and slipped into his apartment to grab his math textbook and the folder containing homework and his attendance sheet. The boys took their cues to move on, but Sam lingered. When Kevin emerged, he could tell that Sam had something he wanted to say.

"What's up, Sam?"

"You remember when I came up here in June, and we went out for beers, and I asked you about the poster I saw of the missing Walker's girl? Did they ever find her?"

Kevin studied Sam's face for a moment and then spoke. "Nah, still no leads. And no body, nothing. I think the police have basically given up. Apparently there's a local P.I. working on it. Why?"

"Oh I don't know, I just can't get the image of the girl's face out of my head. Your kids ever say anything about it?"

"Wait, what are you, an undercover cop or something?"

Sam laughed. "No, why, do I look like one? I'm just curious, that's all. Sorry, maybe it's none of my business—"

Now Kevin laughed. "It's OK, Sam. I'd like to know what happened too. My kids don't mention it very often. I do know that some people here think Tomas Arpante was involved, somehow. And I've heard one of your soccer players badgered his little brother about it."

"Your kids told you that?"

"That kind of incident gets around pretty quickly here."

"But if you really want to play detective," Kevin continued, "You have access to someone who may have more information than my kids do."

Sam looked puzzled. "What does that mean?"

"One of the kids on your hall. A junior, I think. I hear he's seeing a senior at Walker's who may have been good friends with the missing girl."

"Which kid?"

"Warren Cochran. Plays football. Good kid. I don't know the girl's name. ... Gotta get to class. Happy sleuthing!"

Sam was getting to know the kids on his hall through meals and study hall, which he monitored Monday through Thursday, when many of them gathered in the large common room on the second floor of Elephant Dormitory. He knew who Warren was, but hadn't registered a strong feeling for what he was like, other than quiet and studious. Beginning that evening, Sam started paying more attention.

Thursday evening after study hall, Sam, Steve, Joe, and another new young teacher, Mark Lehrer, decided to go out for a few beers. Sam thought of the place they had gone in the summer, but Steve pushed for O'Laughlin's, an Irish place he liked in Simsbury.

The bar was quiet, but the bartender was not; he greeted them with a hearty "How's it goin' there?" in a mild but discernable brogue. "Name's Kieran. You fellas from up the boarding school?"

The men looked at each other. "How'd you manage to guess that?" asked Sam.

"Oh, you had that look about ya," Kieran answered, winking at Steve.

"OK, full disclosure," he added. "I've met Steve on a few occasions. He's no stranger to a pint of Guinness!"

The men ordered pints and carried them over to a square table.

Another party came in. Kieran, who was working the joint by himself, greeted them and took their orders.

"His name isn't Kieran," Sam offered with a mock scowl. "And he's not Irish. He's probably from Iowa."

"Well, aren't we the skeptic," said Steve.

"I don't know that for a fact. But there are lots of fake Irishmen roaming around New England, trying to pick up women with their fake accents and stories of the old country."

The teachers settled in with their pints and traded stories about their students. They got a kick out of Sam's story about Jeff Banks and ZZ Top.

Sam noticed something he hadn't before, and abruptly excused himself from the table. He walked over to the bulletin board near the door, carefully removed the push pins from the poster of Mallory Harding, and walked over to Kieran, who was washing glasses.

"Hey Kieran, what do you know of this?"

He straightened up. "The missing Walker's girl? I don't know much of anything at all. Are you an undercover cop or something?"

"Ha, funny, that's the second time I've been asked that. I'm just curious about this case for some reason. How does she just vanish into thin air?"

"Well, laddie, I think the answer to your question lies in the unlikelihood of the 'into thin air' part of it. Comely young ladies like that don't vanish into thin air. They vanish into some pervert's station wagon. They vanish into a locked basement, or get dumped into a ditch, or into the Connecticut River."

"We're pretty close to Walker's here, aren't we?" Sam asked. "Do their teachers come in here? Does anyone talk about her?"

"Not so much. We see a lot more of you guys. Different demographic over there, nowhere near as many young bachelors."

A voice piped up from the end of the bar, from an older woman, 50-ish, whom Sam had not previously noticed.

"She had it coming to her."

"What?" Sam asked, confused.

"I said, she had it coming to her," said the woman.

"And I said, Victoria, I think you've had one too many Manhattans," replied Kieran.

"What do you mean, she had it coming to her?" Sam asked with irritation in his voice. "I find that offensive."

"She was so ... so ... full of herself," said Victoria, a little unsteadily. "Yeah, that's it, full of herself."

Sam looked at Kieran, who just rolled his eyes.

"And you know what else?" Victoria asked.

"Victoria, I think it's time for me to get you a cab."

"I'm not asking you," she said, shifting her unsteady gaze to Kieran, and then back to Sam. "I'm asking him, the good-looking fellow couple of seats over. What's your name, anyway?"

Kieran picked up the phone receiver and picked out a local cab company from the list on the wall.

"Now where was I?" slurred Victoria. "Oh yeah. And you know what else?"

"No, what else?" asked Sam reluctantly.

"I'll tell you what else. She seemed proud to be a slut. That's it, yeah, proud to be a little know-it-all slut. No wonder she's gone mishing. Exchuse me ... missing."

"What the hell are you talking about?" fumed Sam "You don't know what happened to her. Do you even know her? How would you know her?"

"From the, you know, from the class."

"From the class? What class? Are you a teacher?"

"More like, from the "preshenta—"

Victoria was trying to clarify, but words were getting more difficult by the minute.

"From the preshentasin. The pre ... zen ... ta ... sin ..."

"The presentation?" asked a completely befuddled Sam.

"Victoria, your cab is here."

"Oh Kieran," Victoria sighed. "I'm ... I'm so shorry ... Did I settle?"

"You're fine. Don't worry about it."

The taxi driver, who appeared to know Victoria, helped her into the cab.

"Welcome to my other world," said Kieran.

"Who was that?"

"Victoria Lavelle. Works for the state in some capacity. I think she studied behavioral psychology. Funny how those people are supposed to help others with the things they can't fix in themselves."

"What presentation could she have been talking about?"

"Could be one of the talks she gives coming-of-age high school girls. If she did know that girl, that's probably why."

"Is she always that drunk?"

"No," Kieran sighed. "Not always. I wouldn't let her in if she was. I try to help pace her. But she's had a hard life. Engaged to be married, got pregnant, the young man bolted when he found out. Her parents were strict Catholic, sent her to live with an aunt until she had the baby, then made her give it up for adoption. Never married, no kids, except the one she gave away. Very bitter about the whole thing."

Sam sat back down at the table, still holding the poster of Mallory Harding in his hand.

"What was that all about?" Steve asked.

"Nothing," Sam replied. "Weird, drunk woman trying to pick a fight with me."

I thought she was trying to pick you up," laughed Steve.

"Well, her charm was a bit off tonight."

Joe had noticed Sam looking at the poster in June, and Sam had brought it up once since then. "You seem real interested in that case," Joe observed. "Maybe you can play detective and solve it."

"He just wants to bang her," joked Mark.

"Jesus Christ, Mark," Sam said, smacking the poster on the table. "That's inappropriate on almost every level. I do not want to bang her. She's missing, and let's see, what else ... She's underage."

"Calm down, sorry, I was kidding," said Mark. "But she is beautiful."

Sam took a deep breath. "Actually, Mark, I'm glad you said that. Because if I keep obsessing about what happened to her, that's what everyone's going to think. But that's not it at all. I ..."

Sam hesitated.

"Never mind. You won't understand, and I wouldn't expect you to."

Steve sensed that Sam had something interesting to say. "Go ahead, Sam. I'd like to hear."

"OK, here goes--" Sam paused again.

"When we went to that bar in June, that's when I first saw the poster. Actually, I didn't even see it at first. I felt it."

"Felt it?" Mark looked puzzled.

"Go on, Sam," said Steve.

"Yeah, felt. I felt like someone in the bar was looking at me. A woman. But I looked around at all the tables, and no one was looking back. I realized that the energy I was feeling was coming from behind me. I turned around, and didn't notice anything there, either, so I carefully scanned around the bar one more time.

I thought I heard a soft voice coming from behind me, so I turned to the wall again, and this time I saw her. And the picture froze me. Not because she's beautiful—she is—but because I felt like she was trying to say something to me. Like she wanted me to help her somehow. I'm not kidding you. That's what I felt. And I felt it again tonight when I saw the poster again. And a sensation like that is hard to get out of your head."

Chapter 8

August 1983

Without a call back from the Arpante family, there was little that Jackie Spellmeyer could do in the month of August to work on the Mallory Harding case. She called Simon Savard at the *Courant* to see if he had any more information he hadn't published in the paper yet. He drew a blank, but suggested Jackie pay a visit to Brad Sullivan at the Simsbury PD to see if he had anything else in his notes. That was already next on her list.

Sullivan welcomed Spellmeyer cheerfully into his office, hiding his annoyance that she (so he assumed) was checking up on his thoroughness. "It's pretty much all in the *Courant* story," he said, motioning her to take a seat in one of two wooden chairs in front of his desk. "He picked her up at Walker's after Sunday brunch, and drove her around Simsbury, Avon, maybe West Hartford. He said they went to a mall and a park. A *Courant* tipline caller did say they saw them at one point driving in Avon."

"Do you know which mall? And which park?"

The Simsbury detective bristled at Spellmeyer's laser focus

on specifics. He knew her reputation for details—a dedication to painstaking police work that he couldn't manage to emulate.

"I think it was Westfarms Mall," he replied, sifting through the scant few pages of notes in the Harding folder. "Yes, here it is, Westfarms. New Britain Avenue. On the West Hartford-Farmington line. I'm sure you've--"

"Yes, yes, I know it. What about the park? Is that in your notes too?"

"I don't think so. There are lots of parks in the area. I don't think he specified which one."

"Last thing. Did he give you any details about when and where he dropped Mallory off?"

"Five-thirty. At the school."

"Anywhere specific at the school?"

Brad sighed in frustration. He was beginning to feel like a suspect himself. "At the school. That's all he said."

"OK then," Jackie said. Anything else?"

"Nope."

"Thanks Brad, this has been helpful."

The last full week of August, the Spellmeyers stayed in a rented house in Chatham, on Cape Cod, along with their daughter, her husband, and their two small children. It was an annual tradition they all looked forward to. Jackie enjoyed playing with the kids as much as Maddie and Paul enjoyed the break. That and the soothing sights, sounds and smells of late summer on the ocean kept Jackie's mind (mostly) off of the case.

One late afternoon, they all stopped by Veterans Field to

watch a Chatham Anglers game. They sat in portable lawn chairs, sipped iced tea, and marveled at how the Cape Cod League captured the old-fashioned charm of baseball in a way that no major league game ever could. At one point, Jerry leaned in to say something to his wife. "We don't know a single player out there," he whispered, almost conspiratorially. "In five or six years, a quarter of them will be in the majors."

Jackie couldn't help but picture Tomas Arpante in an Anglers uniform. Their brief meeting had left a favorable impression on her—enough so that she reminded herself that he was still a potential suspect, and she had to maintain impartiality.

After about five innings, restless children signaled it was time to head out for lobster and clam rolls.

With the beginning of school in early September, Jackie wasted no time contacting Reisa Maitlin to set up an interview with Mallory's best friends, Annie Green and Maggie Duchesne. Reisa wanted to give them more time to settle in, but Jackie persuaded her to approach them as soon as possible, and that it might be better to get the interview out of the way before they dug into their studies.

Reisa arranged to have the girls meet Jackie discreetly in an unoccupied faculty apartment. Annie and Maggie, both in plaid skirts and white blouses, walked in with Reisa and took seats around a kitchen table where Jackie was waiting.

"Jacqueline Spellmeyer, very nice to meet you," she said, extending her hand.

The girls nervously reached across the table in turn, clasping Jackie's firm hand and introducing themselves in soft, almost trembling voices. "Maggie Duchesne." "Annie Green." Reisa left and closed the door behind her.

Jackie had been in auditoriums full of teenage students before, in area prep schools several public high schools. Yet there was something about these two girls that stirred in Jackie a wistful reminder of how long it had been since she had been in the full flower of young womanhood, decades ago in her hometown of Warwick, Rhode Island. Annie had a full head of auburn hair, brushed out neatly, spilling down onto her shoulders. Rosy cheeks and sparkling green eyes lit up her face. If she had a cute figure, Maggie was nothing short of voluptuous. She was taller with longer legs than Annie, and big brown eyes and wavy, dark brown hair that looked like it had been teased and styled for a photo shoot. Her demure white blouse, buttoned to the neck, could not hide the shapely front that caused many an Avon boy to forget his manners while talking to her.

Jackie adjusted her glasses and smoothed out the front of her grey skirt. "Well, let's get started. Right now I'm just gathering information," she said, looking up from her legal pad and lowering her glasses to look each girl straight in the eyes. "This won't be an interrogation. As you know, I've been hired by Mallory's parents. So I need to find out as much as I can from the people close to her. Let's see, you're both seniors, right?"

Both girls nodded.

"And maybe ... 17 years old?"

Annie cleared her throat. "I'm 16," she said. "Birthday in October. Now Maggie, she's been 17 since March 29."

Annie, ever quick with a friendly jab, was thinking of saying "17 going on 25," but thought better of it given the serious matter at hand.

"And Mallory," Jackie continued, "I've got it here somewhere that she turned 17 on—"

"April 26," Annie blurted out.

Jackie smiled. "So I guess you are all good friends, right?"

"I guess you could say that," said Maggie, returning the smile.

"Tell me, if you don't mind, how and when you became friends, what you have in common, whether there are other girls in your immediate circle, and so on."

The two friends looked at each other. Their initial shyness about the interview seemed to be giving way to a more comfortable feeling about sharing information with Jackie, who already had guessed that neither one of them was the quiet type. And while Maggie already seemed a little more worldly, Annie appeared by their consent to be the primary spokesperson.

"Well, Maggie and I hit it off, like, the day our parents dropped us off to start freshman year. I mean, like, they pulled up behind is and practically hit our car—"

"We did *not*," Maggie interjected. "Your father didn't know where he was going and slammed on the brakes. You're lucky my mother was paying attention."

"OK, OK," Annie laughed. "So our parents all get out, and I'm thinking there's going to be, like, this big argument, but everybody started apologizing to each other, and next thing you know, we're all laughing about it. And Maggie and

I caught each other's eye, and like, I knew we were going to be best friends."

Maggie nodded and smiled in agreement.

"Where are you girls from?"

"Exeter, New Hampshire," said Annie.

"New York City," said Maggie. "Upper West Side."

"And Mallory—" Jackie began.

"Summit, New Jersey," Annie cut in, like she was on a quiz show.

"Yes," Jackie smiled. "I have that in my notes. What I'm wondering is, when and how did you meet Mallory?"

"Well ..." Annie began, but then glanced over at Maggie, cueing her to take over.

"I don't know if I can pinpoint the exact day," Maggie began. "Annie and I were inseparable from that first day, while other new girls were still sort of figuring it out. I think our close friendship kept some of the other girls at bay at first. I never thought of the two of us as intimidating, but maybe we were."

"I thought Mallory was the intimidating one," said Annie.

"I don't know if I'd say intimidating," Maggie countered, looking up at Jackie. "More like impressive. Confident. And not in a snobby way. She just had an air about her that the other girls wanted to emulate or get closer to. They wanted to hang out with her. And one by one, they tried."

"And how exactly did they try?" Jackie asked.

"Oh ... I don't know, they just tried to get close. Making chit-chat at lunch or in the student lounge ..." Maggie offered, her voice faltering for the first time.

"It helped if you were in classes with her," Annie added. "That's how Maggie and I got to know her. Biology class. We all started making fun of Mr. Price together, and the question he made us try to answer the first day—"

"What is life?" Maggie cut in, and they both laughed.

"The other thing," Maggie said, "was we all did the equestrian program. That was a big way to get to know Mallory. She did make other friends there. Not that she ever liked any of the girls as much as she loved her favorite horses ..."

Annie and Maggie laughed in sync, as if on cue.

"Can you name some of these other girls?" Jackie asked.

"Well, let's see," Annie began. "Beth Hoffman. Suzanne Fiorini. Melissa Clark ..."

"Cathy St. John?" suggested Maggie.

"Oh, yes, her too." Annie confirmed. "She came a little later."

"To Walker's?" asked Jackie.

"Oh, no, I meant to the riding program," said Annie. "I almost got the feeling ..." she paused.

"That she joined equestrian to get closer to Mallory and our group," said Maggie, finishing her friend's sentence. "Cathy was a little shy and awkward at first. Had trouble making friends, breaking into one of the circles of girls. Once she started riding, she seemed to make more friends and get more comfortable socially."

Jackie was taking notes in shorthand, getting all the names, and whatever other details struck her as important or interesting, down on paper. After a few seconds of silence, she looked up from her pad, lowering her glasses again.

"Lots of friends—any enemies?" Girls she didn't get along with? Avon boys who were angry that she wouldn't date them?"

Annie and Maggie looked at each other, then shrugged their shoulders. "I can't think of anyone like that," Maggie said finally.

"Boyfriends?

Both girls smiled.

"Every Avon boy wanted to date Mallory," said Annie.

"And Mallory wanted to date every Avon boy," said Maggie with a barely muffled chuckle.

"She must have been busy then," offered Jackie.

"Well ..." Maggie began.

"Here's the thing," said Annie. "Freshman year, forget it. There are all these rules. And I think—"

Annie glanced at Maggie, not at all sure she would agree with what she was about to say. "I think we were, like, a little too young and silly freshman year to date."

To Annie's surprise, Maggie nodded and continued the thread. "Sophomore year," she said, we were a little more grown-up, and we spent more time with the Avon boys, but mostly in groups. It was almost like a game to see who would break off into pairs first."

Annie smirked. "You had no trouble breaking off into pairs to make out at dances. But it was never the same boy—"

"Shut *up*!" Maggie retorted. "Just because you found your forever sweetheart sophomore year—"

"Late sophomore year. And I didn't start dating Warren

for real until junior year. You, on the other hand, couldn't make up your mind, like a girl at a dessert buffet."

Maggie's eyes flared as she formed her reply, but before she could speak, Jackie cut in and redirected the conversation.

"As entertaining as your love lives are, it's Mallory's love life I need to know more about."

"Well," Maggie began, "by junior year, Mallory really had all the Avon boys under a spell. You know who she reminded me of, Lady Brett in that Hemingway novel. It wasn't just that she liked boys and they liked her—she had power over them, like they practically trembled in her presence."

"And yet she was so independent," Annie picked up, "that she, like, didn't need to settle in with a boyfriend. I think she enjoyed the attention without the commitment ..."

Annie paused as she suddenly remembered something about the first semester of junior year, just one year ago. "You know," she continued, "come to think of it, last November was the only time I remember Mallory being ... well ..."

"Depressed," offered Maggie. "She was always so effervescent. Then all of a sudden, she came back from Thanksgiving break and she seemed dark and withdrawn. It was so not like her."

"You know why," said Annie, searching Maggie's face to make sure they were on the same page.

"Yes," answered Maggie.

"Do tell," said Jackie.

"Her father and mother were considering a divorce," said Maggie. "He discovered she was having an affair. And she was upset with him over money or some such thing. When it got ugly, Mallory withdrew. And her brother just retreated into his social life."

Jackie reflected on the fact that the Hardings had not revealed any of this to her, and immediately thought, why would they?

"She snapped back after a short while," said Annie. "And she was relieved when her parents decided not to go through with the divorce. I give Cath a lot of credit for helping Mallory through this. She gave a lot of her time, and told her stories of her own crazy household, which seemed to cheer Mallory up. I think she really appreciated that."

"Cath?" said Jackie.

"Cathy St. John," clarified Annie.

"So anyway," Maggie said, "it wasn't until December of junior year that Mallory tried out an actual boyfriend."

"Tomas Arpante?" guessed Jackie.

"No, not yet," replied Maggie. "First she dated a guy named Hank Shahinian. Very quiet, hard to get to know, but one of the most handsome boys on campus. A lot of Walker's girls had their eyes on him."

"A lot of Walker's girls," repeated Annie, smirking. "Any-one come to mind?" She glanced over at Maggie.

"Oh *stop*," Maggie said. "Yes, I thought he was hot. But I did not try to steal him from her."

"Anyway, there was no time to steal him," remarked Annie. "They broke up after, like, two weeks."

There was a short silence while Jackie scribbled notes.

"Any particular reason?"

The two friends looked at each other and shrugged their

shoulders. "Hard to say," said Annie finally. "They were dating and then suddenly they weren't. I think Mallory thought, like, he wasn't into the relationship enough. Like he was too aloof or something."

"And once Mallory started dating for real," said Maggie, "she was very passionate about it. When she and Tomas finally got together, sparks flew."

"They couldn't keep their hands off each other," laughed Annie. "The hottest couple in central Connecticut."

Maggie chuckled briefly, then went quiet.

"And this went on through spring?"

"Yeah," Maggie replied, "until the day she—"

Without warning, Maggie burst into tears. Annie reached over and threw her arms around her friend. "Oh girl ..."

"I'm ... sorry ..." Maggie sobbed. "It's just ..."

"I know this conversation isn't easy," said Jackie in a low, soothing voice.

"It's just so weird sitting here talking about her," said Annie, who also was trembling now, with tears running down her cheeks.

Maggie managed to stifle her sobs, but her tears were also flowing freely. "And I don't know whether to use past or present tense. I don't know what happened or where she is. And I miss her so much."

The girls hugged and waited for the tears to subside. "I hope I didn't push you too much," Jackie said apologetically. "But do cry, that's good. Let your emotions out."

"It's OK," Maggie said.

"I was just going to ask you one more thing," Jackie said. "But if we need to stop here, that's fine. It can wait."

By now, Annie had more or less composed herself. "Go ahead," she said.

"When you talk about dating, here at these private schools with their strict rules and busy schedules, what does than mean? What do couples do, and when?"

"Well," Annie said, "the school week is very busy with classes and activities. You don't get to see each other much. Weekends there is more free time, and there are also dances, and like movie nights and so forth. With your parents' permission, you can also leave campus for the weekend, but that can be tricky with a boyfriend. Sunday is the big day. No classes, no sports, shuttle busses are running between the schools, and you have, like, the whole day free."

"Tomas has an old car his parents gave him," said Maggie. "Most Sundays he'd pick up Mallory and off they'd go. You might go to the mall, or to a museum, or maybe a nice park to walk around."

"Or find a secluded spot to park and make out," added Annie. "And whatever else."

"Whatever else?" asked Jackie.

The two girls went silent for a minute.

"OK, Maggie said finally. "It was no secret that Tomas and Mallory were, you know—"

"Doing it," blurted out Annie.

Jackie maintained her even demeanor; allusions to teenage sex were hardly a shock to her. "And then at the end of Sunday afternoon, he'd drive her back to Walker's?"

"Yes." "Yes," they answered in turn.

"At what time, typically?"

"Oh, six or seven," said Annie. "You had to be back by seven."

"Now he told the police he dropped her off at 5:30 that day. But apparently, nobody saw her. Did you normally see her when she got back to campus?"

Another pause.

"I guess it depends," said Maggie. "Maybe if you both show up at dinner. It depends what everybody was off doing before they got back. Or if you're already in your room studying. You're not making a mental checklist of who's back on campus and who isn't. Only her roommate began to worry, and that wasn't until later. The rest of us didn't realize she was missing until the next day."

Once again, Maggie began to sob softly. "I don't know what to do or think any more. I wish she'd just show up safe one day, here or in Summit or wherever, and this would all be over. But I don't think she will. I don't think I'm ever going to see her again."

Chapter 9

September 1983

"Winged Beavers rule!"

The Avon Old Farms J.V. players trotted off the field grinning and giving each other high-fives, having just defeated Loomis Chafee 2-0 and improved their season record to 3-0. Jim Longworth made several diving saves in net for Avon; the goals were scored by Mike Marder and Nico Arpante, both assisted by Graham Toomer. Not only were Toomer and Arpante getting along; they were passing to each other.

"Nice work," barked Coach Field in a brief postgame pep talk. "You found space and stretched the field on offense. That's why we had so many chances. It could have been 6-0."

"Or 4-2 them if not for Jimmy," piped up Bart Bazeby, the central back and unofficial team captain.

"Yes, great job back there, Jimmy. And you too, Bart and the defense. They had a few more good shots than I would have liked, but for the most part, you stepped up and challenged and kept them from getting too comfortable. Coach?"

"Good possession in the midfield, too," added Steve Morrow. "They never really had a chance to take over the flow."

"OK now, over and back," said Sam. "And enjoy your Saturday."

At that, the players jogged across the field and back. As they returned to the side where the home fans were standing or still sitting in folding chairs, they received a sprinkling of applause from a handful of parents and classmates.

One of those parents was Mario Arpante, who singled out Sam for a handshake. Beaming with pride at his younger son's performance, he told Sam, "Mr. Field, I just want to thank for all you've done for Nico so far this season. He's very happy with your coaching and your guidance."

"Thanks," Sam smiled. "He's a good player. And he listens and improves. Oh, and I hear he's not the only athlete in your family."

Mario shot Sam a curious glance. "You know about Tomas? You weren't here last year, were you?"

"Oh, his exploits on the field here at Avon are legendary. And I hear he's at UConn on a baseball scholarship."

Of course, Sam said nothing about the Mallory Harding case, and did his best to convey that the only reason he knew Tomas' name was through sports.

"Well, again, thank you. See you next home game." He looked around for his son. "Nico, you coming with me?"

"Reese, get your ass in gear," yelled Sam, smiling as a chubby boy with a round, freckled face loped around the bench area, humming to himself and picking up loose soccer balls and stuffing them into the netted ball bag.

"My ass is in overdrive," countered the boy.

In just a few weeks, Sam had become very fond of the

wisecracking Reese Gilmartin, a sophomore who was fulfilling his fall sports requirement by working as the J.V. soccer team manager.

"And speaking of gear, can you tell the athletics office to splurge for some more shin guards? We're down to our last spare pair."

Sam lifted the hatch on his Mercury Capri, and Reese tossed in the ball bag with a flourish. "Did you get all the game stats?" Sam asked.

"No, I got the stats for the thirds game over there. What do you take me for—fat and lazy? Don't answer that."

"I suppose you'll want a ride back to the quad."

"No, I think I'll just fly."

Sam parked the Capri in the faculty lot about 30 yards from the quad, where he and Reese got out and started walking toward the dorms. As they turned the corner toward Sam's apartment in Elephant dorm, Reese was the first to notice Warren Cochran, standing in the courtyard near Sam's door with two girls.

"Hey Warren," Reese called out playfully. "Who's the lucky girl this week?"

"Hey Reese," Warren responded, unfazed, smiling sideways at Annie. "I'd like you to meet my girlfriend of, oh, what, a year now? Annie Green."

Reese and Annie nodded at each other awkwardly.

"And Annie," Warren continued, "I'd like you to meet my dorm master, "Mr. Field."

Sam extended his hand and shook Annie's.

"Yes, nice to meet you, Annie," Sam said, "Warren has told

me about you. Not a lot, mind you, just enough to let me know he's crazy about you."

While Annie blushed, Maggie's eyes appeared ready to launch fire darts at Warren.

"And oh my, I'm so sorry to be rude," Warren exclaimed. "Maggie Duchesne, Mr. Field. Mr. Field, Maggie Duchesne."

"And I guess I'll be off now," said Reese, waving one hand as he stepped away from the group. "I'm Reese Gilmartin. But you can just call me chopped liver."

Reese's sarcastic exit brought chuckles from the students. Sam waved after him and said, "Thanks Reese. See you Monday."

"So then," Sam continued, now facing Maggie and extending his right hand. "Nice to meet you. I take it you're a friend of Annie's?"

"Yes, that's right," she answered shyly.

Sam and Maggie looked at each other for a long moment, as an unexpected feeling came over him. Then he changed the subject to stop it in his tracks, breaking the awkward silence.

"Did you guys watch the varsity soccer game?" Sam asked.

"We watched some of your game too," Warren replied. "Nice going, coach."

"And your football game is later this afternoon?"

"Yeah, four o'clock," Warren said.

"And do you girls both go to Ethel Walker?" Sam asked.

"Thats right," said Annie. "We're seniors.

"Ah, robbing the cradle," Sam said, motioning to Warren, who was still a junior.

The girls both laughed, as the awkward tension slowly lifted, though not enough to prevent gaps in the conversation.

Sam took it upon himself to break the silence. "So where's everybody from?"

They all glanced at each other; Warren and Maggie said nothing because they knew Annie would step up and do all the talking.

"Warren is from Albany, New York," she began. "Well, not Albany exactly—Bethlehem. A suburb. I'm from Exeter, New Hampshire, and Maggie is from the Upper West Side. You could say she's from New York City, but if that's all you say, she always clarifies which part."

"That's interesting," Sam said. "I just moved here from New York City. I had an apartment on the Upper East Side. I was working at an ad agency—Young & Rubicam."

"Wow, sounds glamorous," said Maggie enviously. "Why did you leave?"

"Well, it wasn't really glamorous at all—not at my level in the pecking order, and especially not at my salary. And there's nothing glamorous about media planning. I applied to the creative department and ended up crunching numbers."

"Was your apartment nice?" asked Annie.

"My bedroom had no windows," laughed Sam. "I was renting the extra room from a couple who were already subletting. It was originally supposed to be the dining room. They closed up the last wall, and there you are, instant bedroom. But the living room was nice with a big window facing 90th Street. And the couple I rented from were very nice. We're still friends."

"But you're not from there, right?" asked Maggie.

"Nah, I'm from Northampton, Massachusetts. Straight up I-91."

"That's where Smith College is," said Maggie. "My parents took me there on a college visit last spring."

"Ah, good school. All female, but you knew that."

"Oh, Maggie will have no trouble finding the boys," giggled Annie. "I hear there's another school a few miles away ... Let's see, what's it called ... Amherst?"

Annie pronounced the "h" in Amherst, much to the annoyance of Maggie, who quickly corrected her. "Am-*erst*," Maggie enunciated. "Am-*erst*."

"You say tomato—" Annie began.

"No, I say it the right way," Maggie interrupted.

Normally, Maggie would have been quick to pounce on her friend's caricature of Maggie's infatuation with boys. But at this moment, another infatuation was taking hold.

"Girls, girls, let's all get along" sighed Warren, though he was used to their verbal sparring, and kind of enjoyed it. "Has anyone thought to ask Mr. Field where he went to college?"

"Well, OK then, Mr. Field, where did you go to college?" Maggie asked.

"Oh ... um ... Princeton. It's a little school in the middle of New Jersey."

"Well, well, Princeton." Maggie said. "A little school in New Jersey. Hmmm ... more like a renowned Ivy League school in New Jersey. Very impressive. Where did you go to high school?"

As the conversation became more of a back-and-forth

between Maggie and Sam, he began to notice that her dark eyes were focused directly on his, and the sensation he had felt when they were first introduced was slowly coming back. This time, he didn't try very hard to chase it off.

"Northampton High School."

"Oh, okay, you went to public school," said Maggie, who had assumed otherwise. "And then to Princeton. Good for you. Did your parents ever consider sending you to a private school? Like Williston Northampton, or maybe someplace farther away? Just wondering."

"Nope! NHS all the way! Go Blue Devils!" he laughed.

"But seriously, it never really came up. I don't think my parents are inclined that way, and they went to public schools themselves. I'd say they thought Northampton public schools were fine. But my mother was always pushing me to go to Princeton, and making sure I kept my grades up. In the end, I applied to Princeton, and to RPI, where my father went, and to Cornell and Yale. I was accepted to all but Yale. I guess I was annoyed by that, but I didn't really want to go there anyway. When my mother took me to Princeton for my visit, I fell in love with it. So I'd like to think going there was my idea, but it may have been a sinister plot my mother was working on all along."

The group fell silent for a moment, content to listen to Sam talk about his background. He was afraid he was boring them, but all three seemed genuinely fascinated by his story, knowing full well they were not that many years behind him in their own journeys. Maggie, for her part, was still alternately gazing at him and then looking away, embarassed and a little annoyed with herself.

Sam finally spoke. "What about you? Colleges? Anyone applying to Princeton?"

"I've got more than a year to figure it out," said Warren. "My parents took me to Wesleyan when they dropped me off this year. It's not far from here."

"I'm looking in the Boston area," said Annie. "BU, BC, Northeastern, Providence College."

"So far I've only applied early decision to Georgetown," said Maggie. "We'll see after that. Maybe Smith, Williams, Bryn Mawr, or Wellesley."

"I think Mallory was applying to Princeton—" Annie began. Maggie shot her a look, but it was too late.

"Who's Mallory?" Sam asked, although he knew exactly whom Annie was talking about. After all, Kevin had tipped him off that Warren had a direct connection to Mallory Harding through his girlfriend. Sam had already been thinking about how to get Warren to talk about that connection. He had figured it might take a while to bring it up naturally in the course of several conversations, but here they all were laying it out for him on a platter.

"Mallory Harding." Annie sighed heavily as she spoke the name. "One of our best friends at Walker's. But she went missing in early May. Fell off the face of the Earth."

"Oh, I see," said Sam. "I'm so sorry. Actually, I have heard about this—"

He was about to say "case," but didn't like the clinical sound of it. "This ... situation. I've seen posters in a couple of places down in town. Beautiful girl. No posters on the Avon campus though."

"That's because George Dicklehead ordered them all taken down," said Warren.

"Again, I'm so sorry," said Sam. "This must be very hard on you."

You have no idea, thought Maggie.

"It's been a rough year," said Annie. "We're making do the best we can. Trying to concentrate on school, and equestrian, things like that. And just supporting each other."

Memories of happier times with Mallory were now flooding into Maggie's head, weakening her defenses. *I can't let him see me break down*, she thought.

"I just wish there were something I could do," Sam said.

Find her, thought Maggie. *There's something you could do.*

"No one seems to have a clue what happened to her," said Warren. "Not even the police. It's almost like they've given up."

I can't let him see me break down, Maggie repeated to herself.

"Wasn't she last seen with her boyfriend?" asked Sam.

"So, you have been following the case," said Warren, surprised.

"Guys, this is really upsetting Maggie," Annie interjected. "I think we should get going."

He is going to see me break down. There's nothing I can do to stop it.

Maggie was now delirious with emotions that came hurtling out like a freight train. Sobbing, she staggered forward;

Sam was standing in front of her and had no option but to catch her.

"I'm sorry," she said, her head settling into Sam's chest, her hair spilling over his arms, both of her hands curled up to rub her eyes. Sam held her steady with one hand on the small of her back and the other rubbing her reassuringly between her shoulder blades.

"It's OK," Sam said as Maggie's tears moistened the front of his shirt.

"I just wish someone would find her," Maggie said softly as Sam gently began to disengage. Dropping her hands from her eyes, they landed momentarily on Sam's wrists. She wanted to squeeze his hands, but thought better of it.

"Well," Sam said with a sigh. "Again, I'm very sorry about all of this. But very nice talking with you all. Good luck today, Warren."

"Thanks, Mr. Field." He turned to walk away with the girls, then turned around once more. "You're a smart man, Mr. Field. Maybe you can find her."

As he opened the door to his apartment, Sam considered Warren's parting shot. Did he know more about Sam's interest in the case than he was letting on?

Once inside, Sam fell back on his couch, sighed heavily, wiped his sweating brow, and tried to process the various emotions he had just experienced. The chemistry between Sam and Maggie had been palpable—and therefore dangerous. He could not allow that to flourish under any circumstances.

All at once, he realized the difference between the two

17-year-old girls who had somehow, suddenly, managed to burrow their way into his interior life.

In a mere 15 minutes, Maggie had stirred within him a profound but forbidden passion. If it was at arm's length while they talked, it surged through his core when he held her. He couldn't put a name on it, but it felt like the glow of anticipation he had experienced only a couple of times in his young adult life, while flirting with young women he was seriously interested in as potential partners. Why this 17-year-old stranger had made him feel this way he wasn't sure; he knew only that his heart was still pounding. And he knew it was wrong, and needed to be suffocated.

And now the difference between his feelings for the two girls was plain to him. His attraction to Mallory was not about romance or sexual fire. It was about something more spiritual, more ethereal. It was a voice on the wind saying *look for me, help me, find me. Look in the places others are not looking.*

Chapter 10

October 1983

Ani Shahinian parked her BMW in the lot behind George Dickleman's apartment building. She had driven directly from her home on Worcester's West Side, and needed to make a couple of adjustments before going in. She kicked off the flats she had worn for the drive, and slipped a pair of black five-inch heels over her sheer black stockings. She hadn't bothered to put her earrings on before driving; she reached into her purse for the pair she had chosen, and fastened them. She took a small vial of perfume and placed a dab behind each ear, as well as one between her breasts. Then she pulled out her lipstick for a fresh coat, smacking her lips together and dabbing them with a tissue before putting everything back in her purse.

Ani was dressed in a sleek black pinstriped skirt suit over a white silk blouse. She was 5-8 with dark hair, chiseled facial features, and a slender build (apart from her breasts, which she had paid a substantial sum to enhance). It was easy to see where her son got his dark good looks.

Ani unbuttoned a button on the blouse, then buttoned

it, and finally unbuttoned it again. She was looking forward to seeing George, and feeling his athletic body surround hers, but she also liked to tease him slowly before getting down to it, and she wanted her look to be perfect.

George let her in and immediately threw his muscular arms around her. Ani gently pushed him back so she could size up just how happy he was to see her. "Oh, my, George has been thinking about Ani, hasn't he," she cooed, running her fingertips slowly across the front of his pleated khakis. "Well Ani has been thinking about George too," she said as she stepped away and slowly slipped off her jacket, one sleeve then the other, and dangled it in one hand with her other hand on her hip.

"Do you like the pinstripe look?" she asked him. "Ann Taylor."

"Everything looks good on you," replied George, who was all too familiar with Ani's exaggerated foreplay routines. "It looks even better off of you."

"Ha," she replied, throwing the jacket playfully at his face. "All in good time, my darling. Oh dear, I'm so clumsy. My nails must be too long. Can you come here and help me with the buttons on my blouse?"

George complied, unbuttoning and removing her shirt, while Ani unhooked her black bra. Again, George tried to pull her closer, but once again, she pushed him back. She had to call the shots. And she knew it gave him a perverse thrill because in most facets of his life, he was in control of everything.

Ani stood a few feet from George, still wearing her skirt,

stockings and heels, naked from the waist up. She placed both hands suggestively on her hips and smiled. "Well, how do I look now?"

"Sensational," said George. "But you are the queen of the tease."

"I like the queen part."

"I think you like the tease part, too."

"Oh, I *love* the tease part!" she laughed.

"You do remember that we have a 4:30 meeting."

Ani gasped in mock surprise, cupping her hands to her cheeks. "Oh, where *does* the time go," she said. "Well, darling, whatever are you waiting for?"

An hour and fifteen minutes later, George watched from his window until Ani's BMW pulled away, then took a quick shower. He dried off, applied a little cologne to his chest, neck, and wrists, then quickly dressed. It was a familiar routine, but he usually tried to leave himself a little more time to make his next appointment. At 4:15, he pulled away in his Saab to hustle over to the Old Farms administration building.

Kevin Doolan was walking past administration, where he had just noticed Ani and Hank Shahinian going inside. Now he watched as George, looking rushed again, filed in behind them. Kevin smiled; Sam, arriving at the scene, took this all in. "Afternoon, Kevin," he said.

"Must be an important meeting for Mrs. Shahinian to drive all the way from Worcester," Kevin deadpanned.

"Hank wants to do fewer sports and more theater," Sam said. "George doesn't like the idea."

"He wants to do theater, let him do theater," Kevin mumbled, shaking his head.

Sam walked into the meeting room right at 4:30; the others were assembled around a conference table. George sat at one end; Mason Chadwick, an English teacher and head of the theater program, sat at the other end. Hank and Ani filled the two seats on one side of the table. Sam took the only vacant seat, next to Perry Michaels, Hank's dorm master and also Sam's faculty advisor.

"Alright, let's get on with it," said George. "Mr. Chadwick, why don't you explain to the group what Hank has proposed to you."

Mason stood up, clad in khakis and a brown tweed jacket. He was a stout, affable man of 40 who had started at Avon five years earlier and begun a theater program that previously didn't exist. The auditorium was there, but it was used mainly for the daily morning meeting, visiting lectures, and an occasional performance by a local folksinger or string quartet. Mason did the best he could to adapt the stage area to theater; he soon persuaded the school's board to install a state-of-the-art curtain, and to construct an expanded backstage area one summer that included wings and dressing rooms. George was ever skeptical of the program, but parents of students who did theater seemed pleased with the experience, and George, almost reluctantly, began using it as a selling point, much like the new swimming pool and squash courts.

"As most of you know, I had the pleasure of having Hank Shahinian in my program last spring for our production of *A*

Midsummer Night's Dream. It was his first experience with live theater, and he took to it like an old pro. Right, Hank?"

"I-I guess so," stammered Hank, surprised to be put on the spot so quickly. "It was fun."

"A few weeks ago, Hank approached me about the possibility of doing theater for his extracurricular activity in both the winter and spring trimesters this year. I know that's not our usual way of doing things, but it might work out well for both of us. The plays I'm looking at are *Twelve Angry Men* and *Arsenic and Old Lace.* Both have large casts for a small school where most boys are doing sports. I probably will reach out to the Porter's or Walker's drama programs for a combined cast on *Arsenic,* but I need as many boys as possible for *Twelve Angry Men,* and I can't double up on roles like in *Midsummer.*"

"So, to make a long story short, I'd be delighted to have Hank for both plays. Beyond my selfish reasons, I also think Hank thrives in the theater environment, and I can see him continuing this pursuit in college. Therefore, I strongly endorse making an exception to school policy and allowing him to participate in the theater program in winter and spring."

"Mr. Dickleman?"

Mason sat down. George stood up and cleared his throat.

"As you know, the founders of Avon Old Farms believed that a rigorous program of academic study combined with athletic achievement and physical fitness provides each boy with a well-rounded set of tools to take out into the world that lies before him. I am personally committed to making sure that each boy who receives an education here is afforded the full range of opportunities we can offer, and that includes participation in our outstanding sports programs. So ... I am against allowing anyone to choose a non-athletic activity for more than one trimester per school year."

"I agree with Mr. Dickleman," added Perry Michaels. "It's one thing to skip a trimester of sports for something less demanding like theater. But twice in a row, and he's not getting the physical challenges he needs to ... um ..."

At this, Perry trailed off, not sure how to express what he was thinking. Ani Shahinian had no trouble stepping in to take over, as she stood up and finished his sentence.

"What he needs to become a strong, physically fit, well-rounded man," said Ani. "Too much of this theater thing will make you too soft."

"Mom!" snapped Hank angrily. "Why do you always say that? And what do you mean, 'this theater thing'? You and Dad used to go to see theater at the Charles and the Shubert, and you never talked that way about it."

"That's ... different," said Ani, fumbling to explain the difference. "That's ... I don't know, professional theater. Real actors and playwrights who do it for a living. And beautiful old theaters."

Mason Chadwick could only smile at Mrs. Shahinian's unintended support for the idea of theater as something more than a passing "thing."

"Thank you, Mrs. Shahinian," he said, standing up again. "You're right, professional theater is something to behold. The theaters themselves can be grand, or they can be dark little black boxes, or even just a clearing in the woods. But if it's done well, it speaks to you. It moves you, and it makes you think. You leave the theater with more than just a ticket stub and a playbill and a memory of a pleasant night out."

"And where do those professional actors and playwrights come from?" he continued. "Do they spring fully formed from a magic cauldron? Or do they prepare for it, taking classes, doing community theater, interning at summer stock, eventually applying to a professional academy to train with masters? And maybe it all starts in college, or in high school, the first time they gather up the courage to audition for the school play, not knowing if they're even going to like it, but then, perhaps, finding that it opens up a whole new exciting world to them they barely knew existed?"

George stood up again. "Thank you, Mason, your eloquence is worthy of a London stage. Let's hear from Mr. Field, Hank's coach this season with JV soccer."

Now Sam stood up and cleared his throat. "Hank ... seems to be having a good time with soccer this fall. And his play is improving. He also listens well, and is easy to work with. Are you enjoying playing on our team this season, Hank?"

"Um, yes, Coach Field," Hank said. "As sports go, soccer is one of my favorites."

"And do you think you're putting your best effort into it?"

"Well, yes, I try, Coach Field. I know sometimes I could be more aggressive."

"Hank and I have talked about this. Early on, he seemed a little lost, and he was being outworked by most of his teammates. We had a couple of really good talks about it, and he is playing with more focus. I can't ask for more than that. He's not going to tackle aggressively like Graham Toomer or pump up his teammates like Bart Bazeby. But I'm proud of his improvement, and I do really enjoy having him on the team."

"That said," Sam continued, "At the end of the day, I don't know if team sports are where Hank is really going to grow and prosper. We've also talked about how much he likes theater, and his face lights up when he describes it. Maybe we should let him spend more time in activities that nurture his artistic passions. I vote to let him do the winter and spring plays."

Sam sat down. Mason smiled. George, Perry, and Ani looked a little thrown off by the unexpected show of support from Sam. The room was obviously deadlocked three to three. George was inclined to let Mrs. Shahinian's preference carry more weight than her son's, but finally, he stood up and adjourned the meeting. "Let me mull this over before I make a decision," he said.

"I'll see you outside, Hank, and we'll go to dinner," Ani said. "I need a word with Mr. Dickleman."

She had two items on her agenda.

Alone in the conference room with George, Ani sidled up close to him so he could feel her hot breath on his ear. "This afternoon was wonderful, but too short. I have a room at the Marriott in Farmington, in case you can get away later this evening or even tomorrow morning. You can call me there."

"And I'm worried about Hank. I don't think he's gay, but he just doesn't act very masculine. And he's so good looking. And that girl from Ethel Walker was gorgeous. I met her once and she really seemed to like Hank. He had the prettiest girl at the whole school and he let her get away. Of course she ended up with a jock."

"I do wonder what happened to her."

Chapter 11

October 1983

With Avon JV soccer cruising along at 7-1, and the next game not till Saturday morning, Sam asked Steve to run a late-October Thursday afternoon practice so he could run a few "errands." He had some driving around he wanted to do, but first he had an appointment to meet with Thomas Fenton, a licensed private investigator he had located through the Simsbury Chamber of Commerce. While his specialties appeared to be cheating business partners and cheating spouses, he also listed missing persons as an area of practice.

"So, you're here because you have a missing person to track down," said Fenton, looking dapper in neatly pressed grey slacks, a French blue oxford shirt and a bowtie. "So the obvious question is, are you looking to hire me, or are you looking for some free pointers?"

"Well, sir, I--"

"That's okay, Sam—it is Sam, right? I can give you a few minutes of my time and some of the basics of a missing persons investigation. I'll also give you my card, in case you decide you want a professional to handle it after all."

"Now, who is this person, and what's the connection?"

"She's a young woman, sir. Seventeen years old. Disappeared without a trace."

Fenton tilted his head a little and lowered his eyes. "So maybe she ran away. Were you seeing her? Sometimes people go missing"--here he made mock quote marks with his fingers--"when they are simply trying to start a new life somewhere else. Especially if their parents or boyfriends or husbands are overprotective or, god forbid, abusive."

"Nothing like that, sir."

"Well, what is your relationship to her? And you can cut the 'sir' crap and just call me Fenton."

"I don't know her. But I saw the posters and I got a strange feeling she was asking me for help. I actually know some people who know--"

"Strange, indeed. But I think I know who you're talking about. The Harding girl, right?"

"Yes, Mr. Fenton."

"And you said you were a teacher at Old Farms, right?"

"Right."

"Okay, I'll tell you a few things you should know, and then I have to get back to my real work. One: find out everything you can about where she was that day, and with whom, and who saw her, and when. She was riding around with her boyfriend, right? Talk to him. Two: find out who his friends are and talk to them. Find out who her friends are and talk to them. Three: if you can get him to show you the car they were riding in, look at the car—look on it, look in it, look under the seats, in the glove compartment, in the crevices that the seat belts and spare change disappear into. Four: when you find a clue that strikes you as interesting, take it, or photograph it. Examine it, think about it, and ask yourself what it might mean. Five: if you're not getting anywhere, widen the circle."

Fenton stopped talking and smiled.

"That's it?" Sam asked.

"One more thing. Six: the Harding family has already hired a local P.I. to look for her."

"Oh, OK. Do you have his name?"

Fenton paused and looked Sam in the eyes. The young teacher hadn't said very much, but Fenton already had a profile going in his head. Serious, earnest, trustworthy, a little naïve, probably pretty smart, possibly a sucker for a pretty face.

"I have her name. And you're going to pretend I didn't tell you this. Jacqueline Spellmeyer. A top-notch professional. That is all. Good day."

As Sam headed for Fenton's office door, the detective picked up his phone. "Nancy, you can show Mr. Hartsburg in now."

On the same Thursday, in mid-afternoon, Jackie Spellmeyer pulled up in front of Beaver Brook and waved to Reisa Maitlin, who was already walking toward the detective's Volkswagen Rabbit. "Get in," Jackie said. "Let's drive for a few minutes."

The Ethel Walker campus was abuzz with girls making their way to sporting activities, the riding stables, and theater and dance studios. As Reisa climbed into the passenger seat and pulled the door shut, several girls walked by in riding outfits. As they passed the car, Jackie said, "Oh … wait … isn't that—"

"Yes," Reisa said, "The girls you interviewed."

"Annie Green and Maggie Duchesne," confirmed Jackie, whose meticulous mind easily stored, cataloged and remembered the names of people involved in her cases. "Who are the other two girls with her?"

"Looks like Melissa Clark and Beth Hoffman."

"Those are two of the other friends they mentioned as good friends of Mallory," said Jackie. "They also named Cathy St. John and Suzanne Fiorini. Do you know if they're all still friends? Do the other two girls ride?"

"They're all still friends as far as I can tell. Cathy and Suzanne dropped out of equestrian for this year. I think Mallory not being here changed things for some people. From what I've seen, I'd say those two girls took it the hardest. Of course, Suzanne was Mallory's roommate. And Cathy, well, they had been very close at one point, but after Mallory disappeared, Cathy just seemed to cloud over whenever her name came up."

Jackie grabbed a notepad from the dashboard and jotted something down.

"So what's up?" Reisa asked.

"I just want to do a quick drive-around so I can get a mental photograph of the whole campus—especially where the boarding students live and eat, and any other roads that go through the property."

"Is that it?"

"And where a girl's boyfriend might drop her off."

"Uh-huh," replied Reisa. "That's fine, I'll show you whatever you need to see. I know you, and I know you're thorough. I also know that she never made it back here that night."

Jackie let that one go without comment. She knew the details still didn't add up, but she wasn't jumping to any conclusions.

Reisa led her driver around campus past athletic fields, student and faculty housing, arts facilities, maintenance buildings, and the equestrian complex. Back at Beaver Brook, Jackie pulled into a visitor space. She turned the ignition off, then sighed.

"So ... did driving around the campus give you any new ideas?"

"Not really. Is there anything else in the neighborhood I should see?"

"There's not much immediately adjacent to Walker's. Lots of woods. Some residential streets. The only other business in the immediate area is the Cobb Montessori School across Sand Hill Road."

"Well, let's go look."

In two minutes, Jackie was idling the Rabbit in the Cobb School parking lot, which directly faced the Walker's campus. "Any reason he would have dropped her off here?" Jackie asked.

"I can't think of one. Why would he make her walk from here? What would he be hiding?"

"At five-thirty on a Sunday, this could be a quiet make-out spot."

Reisa smiled. Her friend's ability to imagine any possible scenario never ceased to amaze her.

Meanwhile, after Jackie's car passed the girls on their way to the stables, another car pulled up beside them—a Mercury Capri.

"Mr. Field! What are you doing here?" asked Maggie, startled and a little embarrassed.

"I've decided to take up equestrian," he said. "Nah ... I was in town for an appointment, and I thought I'd drive over and see the campus—and see how to get here. I have to come over a week from tomorrow with some of my students to chaperone a dance. I imagine Warren will be coming?"

"Yes," said Annie. "That should be a fun night! Don't be afraid to talk to us! ... Oh, sorry, this is Warren's dorm master, Mr. Field. Mr. Field, this is Melissa Clark, and this is Beth Hoffman. I think you've already met Maggie."

Everyone exchanged smiles, except for Maggie, who was blushing, and whose expression was approaching a scowl.

"Well, see you in a week!" said Sam cheerfully before driving off.

When Jackie got home to Simsbury, she found her husband in the kitchen with an apron on, singing and cooking one of her favorite meals, Asian steak salad. "I left a little early today," Jerry said, "and I stopped by the market to pick up steak, greens, carrots, scallions, red cabbage, cashews, and snap peas. We had everything I needed for the dressing in the pantry. And I toasted some sesame seeds."

Duke was watching Jerry intently from the floor next to

the stove; he trotted over to greet Jackie before resuming his position.

Jackie put her bag on the table and walked up behind her husband to give him a hug. "You are the best," she said.

"Oh, and there are two messages for you. Thought you might be interested in the first one--Mario Arpante. I left his number on the pad next to the phone. Not sure what to make of the second one—Thomas Fenton. Isn't he another detective? The one who tracks down cheating spouses?"

"Yeah, maybe he has some info on you!" Jackie laughed. "I have no idea why he would be calling."

While Jerry stir-fried, Jackie picked up the phone and started dialing Mario's number. She thought he might be working, since he cooked in a restaurant. But he answered.

"Mario? It's Jacqueline Spellmeyer."

"Oh, yes. Sorry it took a while to get back. I know you talked to Tomas briefly, but you called Anna again and said you still wanted to see us. My wife is very nervous about this. But I know my boy is innocent."

"So you'll talk?"

"Yes. Just me, if that's OK. I was hoping you could come around to the house Saturday morning, maybe 9:30? Anna will be working at the opticians' office. Nico will be at the school—he has a J.V. soccer game at 11. Which I'd like to go to, by the way."

"Perfect," Jackie said. "I can be there at 9:30 sharp and wrap up within an hour. Here, just let me grab a pen to write down the address."

"How'd that go?" asked Jerry as he layered the plates

with greens, then stir-fried vegetables, then grilled sliced steak, then a drizzle of ginger-soy dressing, and finally the toasted sesame seeds.

"Oh fine. He seemed nice enough. And confident that his son is innocent. I'm not necessarily trying to prove otherwise, there are just a few things I'd like to know more about. Anna won't be there, which is probably a good thing. I'd like to get a closer look at that car—I wonder if it's there, or if Tomas took it to UConn."

"I don't know," said Jerry, "do you think they let freshmen have cars on campus?"

As he spoke, Jerry tore off a piece of steak and fed it to Duke.

"Well, he's got you in his pocket, doesn't he."

"Ha, both of us, I'd say. I wonder if Mario is a Red Sox fan. That'll be a real conversation starter, the way they're playing. How do you have the two best hitters in the league and finish 20 games out? I guess they don't pay you to investigate mysteries like that."

"No, thank god. This is wonderful, by the way."

The next morning, Jackie called the office of Thomas Fenton and left a message. Fifteen minutes later, he called back.

"Sorry, I was on a call," he began. "How've you been, Jacqueline? Long time no see. Well, I'll get right to the point. I had an interesting visitor yesterday. A young Avon Old Farms teacher named Sam Field. Seemed like he came to pick my brain on how to solve a missing-persons case."

"Oh really. What missing person?"

"One you're very familiar with. Mallory Harding."

"What? Who is this person? Did you get a read on him?"

"Hard to say. He seemed normal, quiet, earnest, obviously a little naïve. He said he saw posters of the girl and felt like she was asking him to find her—whatever that means."

"Asking him to find her ..." Jackie's voice trailed off.

"Oh, one more thing, He started to say he knew people who knew her. But I'm afraid I cut him off. I had a real client waiting in the reception room."

Jackie called an old friend in the Avon Old Farms administration who could look up information for her without breaking her confidence. She was aware of George's impatience with investigators on his campus. She weighed her options, and decided to call Sam's phone number rather than risk an appearance on campus.

She called about halfway between the end of his last class and the beginning of soccer practice. Sam was in his apartment, changing.

"Hello?"

"Mr. Field?"

"Who's calling?"

"My name is Jacqueline Spellmeyer. I'm a private detective. I'm working on a missing persons case—an Ethel Walker student named Mallory Harding. Disappeared in May, would be a senior now, Do you know anything about this case?"

"Well ... Sort of ... A little," he stammered. "Why are you calling me?"

"Well, let me ask you a question. Why were you meeting with Thomas Fenton?"

"Oh, he told you. I just have an interest in the case, for some crazy reason," Sam said nervously. "He agreed to give me about 10 minutes of free advice."

"And what makes you think you can solve this case?"

"Well, I don't know if I can. It's just that every time I see her poster, I feel like she's looking at me, pleading with me to find her. I know that sounds crazy."

"Well, yes, it does!"

"Listen, I never meant to step on anyone's toes," Sam said. "If you want me to drop it, I will. I need to get going soon to soccer practice."

"Well, Mr. Field, do you have any information you'd like to share with me?"

"Not really, I don't have much yet. But one of the kids on my hall is seeing Annie Green, who's a good friend of Mallory's. I've gotten to know her, and another one of their friends, Maggie Duchesne. I feel like the three of them might make a good place to start."

Jackie weighed what to say next. She was a little annoyed, and also concerned that Sam might interfere with her investigation. And she was already a little jealous that he might have access to the students on a more personal level than she did as an older, questioning detective.

"Oh, and I coach Tomas Arpante's little brother. And I've met their father."

Now Jackie was trying to process how Sam already had this much information. "Just curious," she said. "You're new this year, right? How did you even know about Tomas?"

"The eyes and ears on this little campus don't miss much. Now I really do have to go ..."

"OK," Jackie said, pausing, trying not to sound too cranky. "One last thing--If you haven't heard the expression 'Stay in your lane,' well, now you have."

Chapter 12

October 1983

Jackie found the Arpante home easily enough, on a quiet street near the public high school. She pulled in the driveway behind a parked red Honda Accord. There was a two-car garage; the house itself appeared to be a modest-sized ranch. She rang the doorbell, and listened to Mario's sturdy footsteps as he approached the door.

Mario shook Jackie's hand in the entryway and ushered her into the living room. "Sit anywhere you like," he said. "Thank you for fitting this into my schedule."

"No, thank you," Jackie replied, settling into an easy chair. "I appreciate your making the time."

"Coffee? Tea? Anna made some muffins--"

"No, but thank you," she replied. "Do you mind if I take some notes?"

Mario lowered his tall, sturdy frame onto the couch. "Sure, go ahead. Anna tells me you're a retired police detective."

"Yes, about 25 years on the West Hartford force. My husband and I live in Simsbury. I've been hired as a P.I. by the girl's parents in New Jersey. You never met her parents, I don't think—"

"No, that's right. But I did meet Mallory. He stopped by with her a couple of times. Lovely girl."

"How long had they been dating?"

"Oh, maybe several months. He doesn't tell me when a new one starts, and then suddenly she's in the passenger seat next to him."

"Has he had a lot of girlfriends?"

"Oh, I wouldn't say a lot. Two, three, something like that. I think he really liked Mallory."

"Past tense. Do you and Tomas think she's dead?"

"Look, I have no idea. But you don't disappear like that for no reason. Probably some sleazebag cruising the Walker's campus."

"What does Tomas think?"

"He has no idea. At first he couldn't believe she was missing. And he was really broken up over it. As I said, he really liked her."

"Did they ever fight?"

Mario fidgeted uneasily in his seat. "Look. There's something I want to make clear about Tomas. Sure, he's a big, strong, athletic boy. Plays hard at all of his sports—at Avon he played soccer, basketball and baseball. But he's a gentle soul. He would never strike a woman, When he fights with his little brother it's almost always Nico who starts it."

"No, I understand," Jackie responded reassuringly. "And when I met him in July—I believe you know by now that we talked briefly one evening after his game—he did seem like a very nice young man."

"Now, I have one more question about that day," she continued. "Tomas told the police he drove Mallory back to Walker's late that afternoon, but no one remembers seeing her. Do you recall anything unusual about that day? Did you see Tomas when he came home?"

"No, I usually work 2 to close on Sundays. The past few years, I've arranged my schedule around their sports, and they don't have any on Sunday."

"And when you did come home, was he here? Was his car here?"

"He was sleeping. I called out that I had some pizza for him and Nico, but I don't think Tomas woke up."

"And the car?"

"Well, if he was here, the car was here. Look, I wasn't thinking at the time that I was supposed to remember all the details of that day so I could answer questions about them four months later."

"Did he take the car to UConn?"

"Freshmen can't have cars on campus."

"So it's here?"

"Yeah, it's in the garage."

"May I take a look before I leave?"

"Sure. Are we done?"

"Almost. You said he was pretty broken up over Mallory going missing. Do you think he still feels that way?"

Mario thought for a minute. "I'm sure he still feels bad about it. But he's a practical boy, and he has had a very busy summer and fall, playing baseball and getting ready for college. Scouts are looking at him, you know, Let's just say I think he has accepted the fact that he's probably not going to see her again. He has to worry about what's in front of him."

"One more thing. Did Tomas have good friends at Avon?"

"Sure. Once he ..." Mario paused.

"Yes?"

"Yes, he had several good friends. They liked him there."

"It sounded like you were about to say something else."

"No, that was it."

"When he first got there, did he have any trouble fitting in?"

Mario looked at Jackie with an expression that suggested he didn't feel like saying much more.

"Only a little. And only at first. I think he was afraid the rich kids would bully the townie. Of course, that all ended when they realized how good an athlete he was."

"OK, thank you so much for your time. Let's go out to the garage, if you have one more minute."

They both stood up and walked to the door, which he held for her.

"Oh, speaking of townies, does he still have local friends?"

"Oh sure, he still hangs out with a few of them."

Mario opened the garage door, revealing the 1973 Buick Riviera she had seen the night she attended Tomas' game.

"Look, you won't be long, right? I have to go make a call. You can leave the door up when you go, and I'll take care of it.

Jackie walked around the car slowly, taking notes on things like the mileage and the size and location of several dents and scratches. She looked in the windows and didn't notice any-thing out of the ordinary, but she wanted to look under the seats. As a P.I., she was aware of the restrictions on examining private property, but she decided that since Mario had invited her to look at the car, she could look in it, too. Still, she wanted to do it quickly before he returned.

She opened each of the front doors slowly, quietly, and rummaged under the seats, pulling out anything that seemed to merit a closer look. She would have liked to search more thoroughly, but she knew she should wrap it up quickly. And sure enough, no sooner had she closed the last door and straightened up than Mario reappeared at the garage door, looking a little surprised that she was still there.

"I'm all set, thanks," she said, moving toward the driveway.

Jackie had three more questions, but she could tell Mario's patience was wearing thin.

"I'm guessing this was your car before you gave it to Tomas?"

"Yes, that's right. When he got his license. And I bought the Honda you see in the driveway."

"I noticed several dents on the Buick, including a larger one on the passenger-side door—did they happen while Tomas was driving?"

He paused again and looked at her. "I don't know, prob-ably. Why is this—"

"It isn't. It's just my nature to be curious about little things. Thanks again."

Jackie already had guessed that Mario would have fixed the dents during the years he was driving the Riviera. And now, with no collision on this old car with 130,000 miles on it, neither one of them cared enough to spend the money.

She also had decided she would not get a straight answer to her last question, and that it would only irritate Mario further. So she didn't ask him whether Tomas used any alcohol or drugs.

Jackie's two decades of detective experience had taught her to watch for signs that a source is not telling everything, and she already considered Mario to be textbook.

Back in her car, Jackie made note of the one item of interest she had discovered under the front passenger seat: an empty half-pint bottle of Jack Daniel's.

Early that afternoon, Avon Old Farms athletic director Evan Peters was pleased to learn that both the varsity and JV soccer teams had played Westminster to a draw. For years, Westminster had dominated Avon in soccer. This year, they played to identical 2-2 ties.

Walking back to their respective cars, Juan, Sam, and Steve shared their frustrations over missed opportunities, while Reese dragged both ball bags. "Hey, look at it this way, they can't call us a bunch of losers like they usually do."

"We're not losers, Reese," growled Juan. "But we weren't winners today when we should have been."

"Coach Ortega, you know I didn't mean—"

"It's okay, Reese," Juan replied. "I've come to expect, how shall I say, colorful language from you."

"And you too, if you don't mind my saying," Reese said. "I choose only the best in role models, I always say."

Reese knew that being a little sassy with the unpredictable

varsity coach was a gamble, but Juan shot him a sly smile to let him know he wasn't offended. "I hear you're doing a good job as manager," Juan said. "Keep up the good work—we're in the home stretch now. Are you wrestling this winter? Think you can get down to fighting weight?"

"For me, every weight is fighting weight," he replied.

Sam drove Reese back to the quad. To Sam's surprise, Warren, Annie and Maggie were all standing outside Elephant dorm, just as they had been a few weeks earlier. This time, Reese didn't linger.

"Enjoy your foursome," said Reese as he shuffled away.

"What?" said Sam. Nothing Reese said surprised him, but he had to act surprised for the others' sake.

"Just a golfing expression, sir," Reese deadpanned.

"Well," said Sam, turning to his visitors. "Nice to see everyone again. To what do I owe this visit?"

Warren got straight to the point. "Maggie would like to speak to you about something, sir."

"Oh, okay," Sam said, turning to Maggie and smiling. "Speak away!"

"Um ... Annie and I are going to take a little walk," Warren said. "We'll be back in about a half-hour or so." With that, they turned and walked toward one of the corner entryways to and from the quad. They were gone before Sam had a chance to process the fact that he was now alone with Maggie. The quad was relatively empty; Sam was hyperconscious of being seen alone with a Walker's student, but he also wasn't sure that standing outside his apartment with her was the best option. So before he even knew what he was thinking, he invited her inside. She nodded and followed as he unlocked his door and stepped into his living area.

"Have a seat," he said. "Can I get you something to drink? Water? Juice?"

"Sure. Water. Thanks."

Sam went into his small kitchen to get two glasses of water. The living area featured a couch, an easy chair, and a couple of end tables arranged around a table with a TV on it. On a longer table behind the couch were Sam's turntable, cassette deck, receiver, and two modest speakers. His record albums were mostly on the floor in milk crates. Maggie sat in the easy chair.

Sam handed her a glass of water, and sat down at the end of the couch closest to the chair. "So," he began. "What's up? How's school?"

"Oh ... school's fine. Look ..."

"Yes?"

"Mr. Field, I just wanted to apologize."

"Apologize?"

"For my behavior the other day, I mean, a few weeks ago, whenever it was. I didn't mean to—"

"You were fine," Sam assured her. "You were upset."

"I didn't mean to fall onto you like that and make you catch me. I don't want to get you into trouble."

"Oh, it's okay," Sam said. "No one saw or made an issue of it. If they did, I'd just tell them the truth."

The part of the truth he wouldn't tell them was that he liked it.

"And I didn't mean to be bitchy the other day when

you showed up at Walker's. I just wasn't ready for a surprise like that."

There was silence for a long minute or two, as Sam worked on what he wanted to say next.

"Look, I think we're friends now, if that's okay with you and Annie. I'm not your teacher, and I don't work at your school. So we don't have to ..." Sam trailed off because it wasn't coming out the way he wanted. And he wasn't sure he was being honest. But he also didn't want to scare Maggie off, now that she had reached out. Could they become good friends somehow without breaching their schools' ethics codes? As soon as he thought that, he thought to himself, *Who am I kidding?*

Maggie's thoughts were all over the place—from the feeling that she should get up and get the hell out of Mr. Field's apartment to the same desire he had stirred in her a few weeks earlier.

"We don't have to be friends, either," she said, finally, standing up. "Annie and Warren will be back soon. I should probably leave."

"You can stay till they get back, if you want," Sam said. "And I do hope we can be friends."

Maggie turned away to hide the tear that had begun to run down her cheek.

"Maggie--"

She turned around again to face Sam, and now he could see the tears she was trying to hold back. "I'm sorry, Mr. Field. I shouldn't have come."

"Did I say something to upset you?" Sam asked. "I didn't mean to. Here, I'll walk you out."

Sam didn't make a conscious decision to raise his right hand and rub Maggie's back over her wool sweater, but suddenly he was doing just that as they walked slowly to the door. His other hand was on the doorknob when Maggie turned to face him again.

"Thank you for listening to me," she said, leaning in to kiss him on the cheek.

"No problem."

Sam turned the knob and began to open the door, but Maggie pushed it shut again. She had decided what she wanted to do, rules be damned. Her next kiss was no peck on the cheek. She pressed her lips into his, throwing her arms around his neck. They kissed urgently for a half-minute or so, until Sam pulled away and asked, the words choking in his throat, "What are we doing?"

"I don't know," she breathed, gently pulling him back until their lips found each other again. They kissed, lips now slightly apart, tongues asking subtle questions, both feeling helpless in the primal desire that had overcome them.

If Maggie and Sam had lost all sense of decorum, the sirens took care of that. Police, fire trucks, ambulances. They descended on the Avon Old Farms campus with the swiftness of a well-executed military operation. Every student, teacher, and administrator on the premises ran out of their buildings to see what was going on. The authorities had massed around the school's main gymnasium, and had begun to mark off the area with police tape. Perry Michaels ran out of his apartment behind Elephant dorm just in time to see Sam Field emerge from his apartment with Maggie Duchesne. George Dickleman hustled over from his residence, fearing the worst.

Word spread like wildfire, from the students' dorms to the faculty apartments and houses to the boys holding court in front of Kevin Doolan's door. It was George's worst nightmare come true. They must have found Mallory Harding's body.

They had found a body, all right, but it wasn't Mallory Harding.

One of Kevin's boys had snuck in through the back of the gym for a firsthand look and was now sharing the real story with the stunned Avon community.

Hank Shahinian had been discovered hanging from a fixture in the boys' locker room.

Chapter 13

June 1983

I wonder where a year from now will find me. Back here, I suppose, watching over them for another summer, watching over them from up high in the chair, teaching them to swim, hitting tennis balls with them, eating grilled cheese sandwiches on my break. On a sunny day, I love how everything below sparkles from up in the chair, even the children and the young teens. The sun catches their hair just so, and they all sparkle. And their screams don't sound so loud from up here.

What about my screams? Will I still hear them even if nobody else does? Sylvia Plath wrote about "the loneliness of the soul—in its appalling self-consciousness." I think I know what she meant. Will I find someone or something to overcome my loneliness, or at least hide it away for a little while? Maybe there will be a boy, a summer boy, straw-colored hair bleached out in the summer sun, someone to laugh with, someone to comfort me and hold me and smother me with his urgency, someone to moan softly and clutch my shoulders when he takes his pleasure. Then he will kiss me once on the face and he will be gone.

None of them will know my loss, and my soul will continue to grieve, even when I am smiling and pretending to live.

October 1983

Ani Shahinian answered her door at 8 pm on Saturday to find a Worcester policeman and a chaplain standing on her front step. Her first reaction to their announcement was shock and denial. "Are you sure it was him? Are you sure they identified the right person?" she whispered pleadingly.

The officer had been given information on what to say from the Avon police on the scene. He assured Ani that her son had been identified by witnesses at the gym and then by fingerprint match at the police morgue. At that point, Ani began to shriek. Then she collapsed to her knees and clutched the side of the door frame as her shrieks turned to sobs.

Once she composed herself enough to answer questions, they asked if there were other relatives that needed to be notified. She explained haltingly that Hank was an only child, that his father had died 10 years ago, and that she would notify her own mother, the last living grandparent, the next day.

The officer said that she could come to the Avon police station to view and identify Hank's body, but not until sometime the next afternoon.

"Do you have someone to stay with you tonight?" the chaplain asked.

"No," she replied in between muffled sobs. "That's okay. I'd rather be alone anyway."

"Are you sure?" the chaplain asked.

"I'll be alright," she said, knowing that "alright" wasn't exactly what she meant. "I'll go to Avon tomorrow."

The officer handed Ani a piece of paper. "Here's the address of the police station, and directions from 84. And a number to call to set up a time for your visit."

On Sunday morning, Ani tried to make herself as presentable as possible for her unexpected return to Avon. But by the time she had driven 10 miles on the Mass Pike to her exit in Sturbridge, and reached out her window to pay the toll collector, she was crying softly and her mascara was running.

Soon Ani was checking in to the Farmington Marriott again. She was a little early, but a room was ready. She made as little eye contact as possible with the desk clerk, and strolled her suitcase to the elevator herself.

In her room, Ani composed herself and called the Avon police station. "Anytime between three and four o'clock would be ideal," said the captain overseeing the morgue. "Does that work for you?"

Ani looked at her watch; it was a little after two. "I can do that. Who should I ask for?"

"Captain Harrigan."

"Okay. See you soon."

Ani ate some crackers from her room's minibar, then flushed her eyes and began reapplying her makeup.

Before she left for the morgue, her room phone rang. George and Ani hadn't spoken since the news, but he knew she was back to ID her son, and assumed she would stay at her usual hotel. He asked Ani how she was doing and said he was deeply sorry.

"I'm as shocked as everyone else," he added. "And I don't know what to say or think. I wanted to call you last night, but I didn't know when you would get the official notification or what kind of shape you'd be in. I was thinking of you all night, and how awful this must be for you."

"Thanks George. I don't think the shock has worn off yet. I feel like a zombie at this point."

"If you need to be alone, I understand," he said. "But if you'd like some company for a little while, I can make myself free for dinner."

Ani thought it over for a few seconds. She wasn't feeling the least bit romantic, but she thought a drink or two and dinner with George would be a nice diversion. She accepted.

On Sunday at about 5:30, as Sam was getting ready to head over to the refectory for dinner, his phone rang. It was Warren.

"Mr. Field, I wonder if I could ask you a favor."

"Oh, sure, ask away."

"The last shuttle leaves Walker's shortly, and I was hoping to stay a little longer with Annie."

"So ... you're at Walker's now, and you'd like to stay later. Except you won't have a ride home, unless--"

"Yes, that's the favor. Is there any chance you're free to ... um ... pick me up?"

Sam paused and thought about it for a second. It wasn't as if he had any big plans for the evening—maybe a TV movie, maybe a hockey game.

"What time are you thinking?"

"Eight-forty-five? That way I'm back by nine."

"Okay, I can do that. Where will you be? I still don't know the Walker's campus very well."

"Pull up on the main circle, in front of the building they call Beaver Brook. I'll be nearby, and I'll see you."

Sam pulled in front of Beaver Brook at the appointed time, but saw no one in front of the building. Then Warren and Annie stepped out from the shadows to his left, holding hands. They gave each other a long kiss goodnight, and then she skipped away, giggling.

On the ride home, Warren asked how it had gone with Maggie before the police and ambulances came.

"Oh, fine, I guess. She apologized, and I told her she didn't have to."

Same glanced from the side of his eye at Warren, not sure if he knew more and wasn't telling.

"Oh, by the way," Warren added, "Annie wants to talk to you about something. I think it has to do with Tomas and Mallory. She wants to tell you directly without Maggie around, because she still gets so emotional. I have an idea what it is, but I'll let her tell you."

"But where and when will I see her?"

"At the dance you're chaperoning this Friday."

"Did you guys talk about Hank at all?"

"Not much to say. Very sad. I don't know anyone who knew him on more than a surface level. Kind of kept to himself."

At dinner in a quiet Farmington restaurant, George and Ani mostly kept to mundane subjects and shied away from the obvious one. It was trickier for George, because he was trying to avoid any reference to school life or students. Ani, still dazed, said anything that floated into her head. At one point she did admit that she hadn't even begun to process what Hank had done or why, or whether she even believed it was a suicide.

George drove Ani back to the Marriott, walked her to the lobby, and gave her a quick kiss goodnight. He knew she wasn't ready to be intimate again, but he told her he hoped she wouldn't leave right away. She reminded him that there were affairs to sort out—at the very least, what to do about Hank's belongings. But she would have to get back to Worcester before the end of the week to make funeral arrangements.

As they talked, an idea was forming in George's head. It was an unusual one for George, who was not usually pro-active about tending to other people's feelings, or about draw-ing further attention to a messy situation. But he genuinely wanted to help Ani find some measure of closure.

With the goal of reaching greater clarity around Hank Shahinian's death and the events leading up to it, George called a meeting for Tuesday afternoon. It was to be an "in-formation exchange," not a press conference, and he told his friend Simon Savard from the *Courant* that he could attend with the understanding that it was off the record.

George requested attendance by those present at the meet-ing about Hank's extracurricular activities: Perry Michaels, Mason Chadwick and Sam Field. He invited two Avon offi-cials in to give briefings: Chuck Fanto, one of the responding officers, and Medical Examiner Elizabeth Logan. George also reached out to the two detectives he knew to be working on the Mallory Harding case, Simsbury Police Detective Brad Sullivan and private investigator Jacqueline Spellmeyer.

George called Ani to inform her of the meeting, adding that he didn't expect her to be there in her time of grief. She thought it over and decided to come anyway.

George arranged for the meeting to be held discreetly in the Avon Old Farms chapel.

Despite the somber nature of the occasion, there was an air of collegiality for 10 minutes or so before the meeting officially began, as old friends and professionals who had worked together in the past shook hands and exchanged pleasantries. George and Simon embraced. Jackie chatted with Simon and Brad, and sought out Ani to express her condolences. Ani and George hugged briefly, then kept a respectable distance, though Ani occasionally glanced his way.

Jackie introduced herself to Sam. "I hope I wasn't too caustic on the phone," she said. "I do appreciate your interest in the case."

"I guess it's cases now," said Sam. "I'm sorry, I didn't mean for that to sound—"

"No, you're right, actually," Jackie replied. "Although watch them, they may try to link the two."

"OK, we'll see. In any event, I totally understand that you wanted to make sure I wasn't meddling in your work."

Medical Examiner Logan stepped up to the lectern. The other participants took seats in the benches facing her.

"As all of you know," Logan began, "Hank Shahinian was found hanging in the locker room of the Avon Old Farms School gymnasium on the afternoon of October 22. Based on my examination, I have ruled the cause of death to be asphyxiation, with the time of death approximately 1:45 pm. Officer Fanto can provide any other relevant details. Officer?"

Chuck Fanto stepped up. "A chair was found on its side next to the body. Although one might surmise it could just as easily have been kicked aside by someone other than the victim, based on other evidence, including the lack of fingerprints on the boy's clothing, and the fact that there were no signs of a struggle, we have ruled this a suicide."

"If it was a suicide," asked Simon Savard, "did he leave a note? Do we have any idea on his motive?"

"We have not been made aware of any note," replied Officer Fanto. "As for motive, I think, at this point, we should stay away from idle speculation."

George Dickleman stood up. "I second that," he said. "We don't know what this troubled young man was thinking, and I would remind my good friend Mr. Savard that we are off the record today."

"On the other hand," said Fanto, "we are aware that the Avon faculty present today held a meeting recently to discuss Hank's preference to spend more of his extracurricular time doing theater rather than sports. Is there anything we need to know about that?"

"I'm not sure there is," offered Mason Chadwick. "We hadn't even resolved the issue by the time of the boy's death. I'm Mason Chadwick, an English and theater teacher at Avon. All I know is that when Hank was in my theater program, he was happy and got along with everybody."

"And maybe not so happy or easy to get along with when he was forced to play sports?" asked Brad Sullivan.

Sam Field stood up. "No, that's not an accurate way to put it. At least not this fall. I'm Sam Field, and I have him--" Here, Sam choked on his words and fought not to tear up as he corrected his verb tense. "I had him in J.V. soccer. He was a little awkward at first, but he worked very hard to improve. He and I talked a lot, and even though he wasn't an aggressive player, he learned to fit in on the team."

"But that's just it," said Ani. "He always had to learn to fit in. He was always too soft. He had the prettiest girl at Walker's, and she broke up with him. He needed his father to make him more of a man. If only David had lived--" Here Ani broke off in soft sobs, which she stifled as best she could.

Simon stood up and turned to Jackie. "Mrs. Spellmeyer," he said, "I understand you're working for Mallory Harding's parents. That's probably why you're here. Do you think there's a connection between Mallory Harding and Hank Shahinian's suicide?"

"There's no connection," Sam blurted out, more forcefully than he had intended.

Simon turned toward Sam and sized him up. "So," he smiled, "the J.V. soccer coach-turned-detective has concluded beyond the shadow of a doubt that there's no connection between a missing girl and a boy who was found hanging—even though the two of them were once romantically involved. Interesting. And you might be right. But what's your evidence? We in the reporting business—and the detective business—do tend to form our conclusions based on evidence."

"I ... I ... just know they're not connected," Sam stammered. "I knew Hank. And I know a few of Mallory's friends. I know their stories, and I have a strong sense they don't connect in that way."

"Almost like a sixth sense," he said, trailing off.

Before Simon could respond, Jackie stood up. "I tend to agree with Sam on this. And yes, we in the detective business do form conclusions based on evidence. But for me, that works the other way around. If I don't see evidence that there is a connection—and I don't--then I work from the assumption that there isn't a connection, until I see new evidence that says otherwise. So I come at it from a practical standpoint, even if Sam here"--she turned and smiled at him--"comes from a more mystical one."

"Hank tended to keep quiet about things," offered Perry Michaels. "Maybe the fact that he couldn't make Mallory fall in love with him has been eating away at him all these months."

"Maybe he had hoped to summon up the courage to ask her out again at some point," mused Brad Sullivan. "Tomas would have been off to college this fall. Hank could have tried again, maybe gotten it right. But then she went missing, and that hope was dashed."

Sam was steaming over this new line of reasoning, and he sighed heavily each time a new "maybe" suggestion was made.

Now Ani piped up again. "I think he was overwhelmed by her beauty. Maybe he didn't think he was manly enough to handle her. I think she made him so uncomfortable that he didn't think he was worthy of her."

"That's enough," Sam exclaimed as he stood up, smacking his notebook against the bench, and began striding toward the door. Before he opened it, he turned and faced the others, who just stared at him. Sam's voice was trembling, but he articulated his words forcefully.

"Has it ever occurred to anyone in this room," he said, pausing to take a deep breath, "that maybe Mallory was not the person in the relationship that Hank was uncomfortable with?"

With that, he opened the door and then slammed it behind him.

Silence hung over the chapel like a shroud. George Dickleman and Perry Michaels looked confused. Mason Chadwick lowered his head into his hands and began to weep. Ani's face first went blank, until all the years of denial flooded through her and flushed her face red. She remembered David taking her aside one night, not long before he died, when Hank was only six, a happy child sitting on the rug and playing with his stuffed animals. "I've noticed some things about Hank," David said, "and I've read up on them a bit. Don't be too surprised--"

"Don't be silly," she had told him. "He's not even old enough to know."

"Oh, he knows, even if he doesn't know he knows. That's why I wanted to mention it to you. Just in case. I want Hank to grow up knowing that whoever he is, we love him and we'll support him all the way."

In a flash, Ani realized what Hank needed from his father, and might have gotten, had he lived: not for David to help

Hank become more manly, but to help provide a loving and supportive household where it was okay to be gay.

George had called the meeting to help Ani move toward closure, and in a way he didn't expect or even understand, he had succeeded.

Jackie Spellmeyer stared at the door, thinking about Sam. She was now much more impressed with him—with his insight and empathy, and his apparently native ability to connect dots others could not. She decided to call him and invite him to assist her on the case as much as his schedule would allow.

Chapter 14

July 1983

We ate clam rolls this evening and drank cold bottled beer and talked at the beach. It was nice. I like him well enough. Next time it might go further. I don't love him, but sometimes I need to be held and feel desired and feel a boy give in to me. It's nice to feel wanted like that, with something that passes for love, even if it doesn't last. And it won't last.

Emily Dickinson said thinking of love made her heart grow full and warm. "I can feel a sunshine stealing into my soul," she wrote, "and making it all summer, and every thorn, a rose." She was optimistic.

How can I be optimistic when I can never have you? When I can never love you? I did love you, but you didn't love me back. So there was never any sunshine stealing into my soul. I could smell the rose, a faint, distant, sweet scent, but I could sense the presence of the thorn too. Don't get too close. Because this rose will prick you and your soul will never heal.

When night falls on this place, I have nothing left to hold. And everything I ever wanted passes through me like a whispering ocean breeze.

October 1983

On Friday evening, October 28, Sam Field drove an Avon school van into a visitor parking lot at Ethel Walker School, and parked next to the van Joe Grisman had driven there just ahead of him. Besides a vanload of students, Joe also had Juan Ortega riding with him, which probably kept his vehicle a little quieter than the one Sam had driven. And it was no less boisterous as they prepared to disembark—especially with Jeff Banks and Chet Hennessey in the mix.

"Boys, quiet down," Sam pleaded. "I have to go over the rules before anyone can get out."

The din simmered down to a murmur, which only made it easier for Hennessey to act up. "Mr. Field, you better keep an eye on the Boofulingus Brothers tonight," he said. "You never know what they'll--*ahem*—get into."

"Okay, Hennessey, that's enough." Gabriel Thomas and Zack Curtis were day students and best friends who stuck together and didn't interact much with the boarders; Hennessey's nickname obviously was intended to question their masculinity.

"Mr. Field, do you boof?" Banks asked loudly, with a straight face. The rest of the van erupted in laughter.

"I don't know, Banks, what's boofing?" Sam replied, also with a straight face.

"It's farting," said Hennessey. Once again, the boys in the van let out whoops of laughter.

"Okay, we're wasting time here," yelled Sam. "Quiet down

so I can read you the rules. Then I'll get out first and come around to the passenger door so I can check off your names as you leave the van one by one."

"The dance ends at 10:45, which means this van leaves at 11 sharp. While you're inside, there is to be no foul language. You are to treat the young ladies with respect. Mr. Ortega, Mr. Grisman and I will be watching you. You may leave the building to go outside, but you are not to go far, and you are not to use alcohol or drugs. Understood?"

This was followed by a smattering of *yes-sir*s.

"Okay, I'll meet you at the passenger door. Don't get out until I check you off."

Sam stood at the door of the van with his clipboard, marking off names one by one. When Warren Cochran appeared at the door, he said, "Mr. Field, you know that 'boofing' does not mean 'farting,' right?"

Sam smiled. "I'm familiar with the word. And it's not too hard to follow the etymology."

Once inside the large room set up for the dance, the teenagers followed a familiar pattern: While most of the Walker's girls watched from the far side of the hall, most of the Avon boys filed in and stayed in clusters on the near side. Warren Cochran and a few other boys walked across to join their girlfriends. A DJ was spinning at one end, and several Walker's girls were dancing with each other to "Hungry Like the Wolf" in the middle of the room.

Slowly but surely, boys and girls began to mingle and talk. Eventually they ventured out onto the floor in pairs to dance. Now it was "She Works Hard for the Money." The night was young, and the DJ was waiting for the right moment to spin his first slow song.

Juan, Joe and Sam were still together, chatting, in the same place they had staked out when they arrived. "Should we split up and watch different areas?" asked Sam.

"I suppose if you want to," Juan replied. "It's not like they're going to try much of anything in here. The action will mostly be outside," he said, grinning.

"I suppose," he added, "we should take turns taking a walk around the building every half-hour or so. "We don't want to give them a chance to drink or smoke pot."

"What if we catch a couple making out too hot and heavy?" asked Joe.

Juan chuckled. "You want to stand in the way of biology?"

"Speaking of which," he added, "Look at them. Young and beautiful, almost grown women, ripe like fruit in summertime. You single young men should go and ask them to dance!"

Sam and Joe recoiled at the suggestion. "I'm sure that's not what the Walker's administration had in mind," said Sam, "when they asked Avon to send a few teachers over as chaperones."

"Oh, young teachers these days," said Juan, shaking his head and smiling. "I said ask them to dance, not make out with them. They'd be very impressed if you know how to jitterbug."

Sam shifted to a corner of the room where he was more or less alone, until Annie and Warren walked up. "Hi Mr. Field," she said.

"Hi Annie," he replied. "How are you?"

"Oh, I'm fine," she said. "Have you seen Maggie yet?" Her eyes twinkled when she asked the question.

"No, not yet," he replied. "Is she here?"

Sam hoped he didn't sound too eager. He didn't know how much Maggie had revealed to her friends. He had been thinking about the fact that he would probably see her, and the unexpected thrill of their last encounter was fresh on his mind. But he also knew he had to ease out of a potentially troublesome situation, and he hoped he could trust Annie and Warren. At the very least, Sam figured he could keep Warren in his pocket by offering rides when he needed them.

Several girls were walking past until Annie called out to them. "Hey girls, what's the story? Any good prospects tonight?"

"Wouldn't you like to know," said Beth Hoffman with a sly grin.

"Oh, what does she care?" said Melissa Clark. "Annie has Warren wrapped around her finger."

"Yes, I guess I do," replied Annie, smiling and curling her arm around Warren's waist. "Oh, by the way, this is Mr. Field, Warren's dorm master. Mr. Field, this is Beth Hoffman, Melissa Clark, Cathy--"

"Yes, we met last week, remember?" interrupted Beth. "You drove up when we were walking to equestrian. Melissa, Annie, Maggie, and me. You were driving a Mercury Capri."

"Ah, good memory," said Sam. "Well, Beth, Melissa, nice to see you again. But I don't believe I've met--"

"That's Cathy St. John and Suzanne Fiorini," interjected Annie.

"Hi, nice to meet you too," said Sam, as both girls smiled shyly and said "You too" in voices barely audible above the music. The other girls began inching away until Annie broke the awkward silence.

"Oh, I almost forgot. Suzanne, I think Mr. Field is from your neck of the woods. Don't you live in South Hadley, Mass? Mr. Field is from Northampton."

"Ah, South Hadley!" Sam exclaimed. "Nice little town."

"You think so?" Suzanne replied. "Emphasis on 'little.' Not much going on."

"Oh, I wouldn't say that," Sam replied. Not with Mount Holyoke College there. Then you have the Odyssey, one of the coolest bookstores anywhere. And I happen to think the College Inn is a fun bar."

"You know the C.I.? Doesn't Northampton have way more bars than South Hadley?"

"Well, I dated a woman off and on who went to Mount Holyoke. In fact, I was just--"

A fond memory of Katie flashed across Sam's mind, taking him by surprise, and breaking his train of thought in mid-sentence. Annie, who already seemed to read Sam pretty well, picked up on his moment of wistfulness.

"I have a feeling you still miss her, Mr. Field," she said. "What happened?"

"Oh, long story," he said. "We actually started dating in high school. We were pretty close for a while, and we used to talk about her going to Holyoke and me going to Amherst.

Maybe that wouldn't have been a good idea. But I don't want to bore you girls with the story, so--"

"But you went to Princeton," Annie said, ignoring Sam's concern about boring them. "Did you apply to Amherst? Was it your choice not to go there and be near her?"

Sam sighed and looked at Annie, wondering why she was so interested in getting this information. Maybe it was because college was looming as a potential disruption in her own love life. Or maybe this was just how she is.

"In the end, I didn't apply. Our relationship was getting rocky, and I didn't want to have to make that choice. And yet, we kept falling back into it over the years, several times. I do think it's over now."

"But you miss her?"

Sam looked around at the group. "Aren't you girls bored by now?"

Actually, they all looked intrigued. Maybe it was the fascination of a glimpse into an older man's love life. Or maybe it was the skill with which Annie got him to keep talking. Or maybe both.

"Yes, I miss her from time to time. And I might see her over Thanksgiving when she comes home from Boston. You, Annie, should become a reporter or something. Now, where are the rest of you from?"

To no one's surprise, Annie took the lead. "Beth is from Scarsdale New York, Melissa is from Groton Connecticut, and Cathy—well, let's just say that she's the only one who takes a ferry home!"

"A ferry!" exclaimed Sam, turning to look at Cathy, the

only blonde in the group. "What, do you live on Martha's Vineyard?"

"No." Cathy smiled. "Northport, Long Island. I take the ferry from Bridgeport to Port Jeff."

"Yes, I know it," said Sam. "Now, I know you aren't allowed to keep a car on campus. Does one of your parents bring a car over on the ferry each time you go home?"

"No, I take the bus from Hartford to Bridgeport to board the ferry, and one of them is waiting on the other side. Only at the beginning and end of the school year do they bring the car all the way over, you know, with my stuff."

"Interesting," Sam said. "Now, don't let me keep you all any longer. Go have fun."

"Well, enjoy your evening, Mr. Field," Warren said. "We'll try to be good."

Annie elbowed Warren in the side, and then all six of them walked on.

Sam took his turn circling Beaver Brook and the cluster of buildings connected to it. It was a cool night, and most of the kids stayed inside. He noticed a boy and a girl huddled in the shadows at the side of a building, holding each other under their coats and kissing. Then, turning a corner, he happened on a cluster of Avon boys seated on steps. There was a flurry of movement, bodies rearranging, an object hidden behind them that someone appeared to stab against the concrete and then fling into the bushes. Sam could smell tobacco.

"You know that's against the rules at both schools," he said.

Sam recognized Banks, Hennessey, Graham Toomer, Reese Gilmartin, and a few others.

"Mr. Field, have you caught anyone making out yet?" asked Banks. "They're everywhere."

"Except here," observed Reese.

"Mr. Field," said Hennessy, "we're thinking of having a Devil's Triangle tonight. Is that against school rules?"

"Devil's Triangle," Sam repeated. He thought he knew what they were talking about, but he really didn't want to pursue it.

"It's a drinking game," said Banks, as the others howled with laughter. "Think Quarters."

"Drinking is against school rules too," said Sam. "As for your little game--"

He trailed off, not wanting to give the conversation any more oxygen. "Just remember to be respectful of the young ladies at all times. I'll see you later at the van."

As he walked away, Sam heard Reese pipe up: "Don't worry, Mr. Field, to have a Devil's Triangle, they'd need a girl," he said. "And from where I sit, that ain't looking good."

As Sam made his last turn toward the front door of Beaver Brook, he noticed another couple making out in a doorway. He tried to pretend he did not see them, but he suddenly felt he recognized the girl—maybe one of the ones he had seen with Annie, he thought. Then it hit him. It was Maggie.

The realization dawned on both of them at the same time. Maggie pulled away from the boy and turned her face to the door. Sam lowered his head and walked faster. His heart began to pound. He tried to put what he had just seen in perspective. "That is exactly as it should be," he told himself.

Inside, Joe Grisman observed the odd look on Sam's face,

and said, "Man, did you just see a ghost out there? I've heard stories--"

"No. I'll be fine," Sam said. Juan walked up. Sam told them some of what he had seen on his rounds, including the couples—not named—he had seen making out.

"Let them make out," Juan said. "It's nature. You're only 17 once."

"What time is it?" Sam asked, even though he was wearing a watch.

"Nine forty-five," said Joe. "One hour."

Sam, still flustered by his encounter with Maggie, remembered that he had one more piece of business to conduct.

It took some poking around the big room and side hallways, but Sam found Warren and Annie again. He approached them and began to speak. "Didn't you say--"

"Yes, yes," Warren said. "Annie has something to tell you. I'll let you guys take a walk."

They walked out a side door and sat down on some steps. The area was brightly lit, and Sam made sure they sat well apart from each other. Sam briefly considered, then decided against, trying to smoke out what Annie knew of his behavior with Maggie.

Sam still felt a twinge of jealousy at having just seen Maggie making out with a boy, but he fought it off and glanced at his watch. "Okay, we don't have too much time. What did you want to tell me?"

Annie cleared her throat. "There is something Maggie and I know about Mallory and Tomas that we didn't bring up to anyone because we didn't, like, want to get people in trouble."

She thought for a second about what to say first.

"It started one Sunday evening when I was leaving play rehearsal at the theater, and I saw Mallory crossing Sand Hill Road toward Walker's. She didn't see me that night, and I didn't mention it. But I couldn't figure out why she'd be walking that way. The only thing over there is a Montessori school."

"Then, another Sunday, it happened again. This time I stopped her and asked. She was funny about it at first, looking around, like every which way, to make sure no one could hear her."

"She finally explained that Tomas felt an incredible amount of pressure to succeed at Avon, both in class and at sports. Sunday was the only day he didn't have either, and he had developed this habit of drinking to blow off steam. Sure, he would drive around with Mallory, then they'd end the day parking somewhere and having sex. Some Sundays—not every Sunday—he would be half in the bag when it was time to go home. They had an agreement—either one of them could decide he was too drunk to drive, and Mallory would drop him off at his house and drive herself back to Walker's. She would park in the Montessori school lot across the road, leave the key under the mat, and he'd somehow get to that parking lot to pick up his car early the next morning."

"Holy shit," said Sam, wheels in his head turning. The new information was provocative, but it still didn't add up in a way that would solve Mallory's disappearance.

"Mr. Field, what do you think?"

"I'm not sure, Annie. This is new information. It adds

another layer to the puzzle, but I'm not sure how it fits in. I'll have to think about it."

"Do you think this might help you figure out what happened to Mallory?"

"Not yet, Annie, not yet. There's still a missing piece or two."

Just then Maggie appeared in front of them.

"Well, isn't this cozy," she said.

Sam and Annie stood up. "I'll go find Warren," Annie said. "I think you've got about 20 minutes before you have to drive them back."

Sam and Maggie stared at each other a long minute. Sam finally spoke.

"Cozy as a bug in a rug," he said, smiling.

"Well, how's your night going?" she said.

"Probably not as well as yours, but I did catch some of my kids smoking."

"Not as well as mine? What's that supposed to mean?" Maggie crossed her arms and fixed her stare on Sam's eyes again.

"Oh, nothing, I just mean you're probably having more fun than I am."

"More fun, eh?"

"You know, dancing, hanging out with your friends, talking with the nice Avon boys, and so forth, while I'm dealing with the usual sarcastic bullshit from Banks and Hennessey."

Maggie laughed and rolled her eyes. "All talk, those two."

Sam smiled. "Juan Ortega did tell Joe and me we should ask the girls to dance."

"Well, did you?" Maggie smiled mischievously.

"We didn't think--"

"Didn't think what? That they'd say yes?" Maggie laughed. "I crack myself up sometimes," she said.

"No, I didn't think people would find it appropriate."

"Oh, I see," she said, curling her lips into a vaguely provocative half-smile. "Dancing, not appropriate. I suppose I could think of worse things."

"I'm sure you could," Sam said, half-smiling back at her. "Anything come to mind?"

"Oh, I don't know, drinking, smoking ..."

"There must be party games boys and girls play," offered Sam. "I wouldn't remember, it's been so long ..."

"Surely you don't mean the ones you play at a birthday party hosted by your mother," said Maggie.

"No, aren't there naughtier ones you play when you're older and your parents aren't around?" asked Sam.

"Naughty games," Maggie said, raising her hand to her mouth in mock dismay. "Sounds positively obscene. You mean like Twister?"

Is she goading me to bring up Spin the Bottle? wondered Sam. Because that leads to kissing. Nope, not gonna do it.

"By the way, I met more of your friends tonight," he said, deliberately changing the subject.

"Oh really," Maggie replied. "Which ones?"

"Well, there was Melissa, and Beth--"

"Yes, but I think you met them that day you drove up--"

"Ah, so I did. There also was Suzanne, and Cathy."

"Lovely group of girls, don't you think?"

"Well, sure, yes, if you put it that way."

"Anyone catch your eye?"

"Oh, come on, I'm not here to scope out teenage girls."

"Oh, you're right, you're here to make sure teenage girls don't get into trouble with teenage boys."

If that was meant to be bait, Sam wasn't taking it. "Actually," he said, "Juan almost seems to want teenage girls and boys to get into trouble, if you know what I mean."

She laughed. "Yes, everyone knows about Mr. Ortega."

A pause in the conversation only intensified the tension between Sam and Maggie, as they locked stares again. He felt like she was playing chicken with him, goading him to bring up what they both knew—that he had seen her making out with an Avon boy. But he wasn't going to do it.

"I think my time is almost up tonight," he said finally.

"Well," she replied, still staring into his eyes, "It's been nice talking."

"Yes, it has, hasn't it."

Maggie paused another long minute, looking away and then looking back. Swinging her head away and back again caused a lock of her dark brown hair to tumble in front of one eye, almost as if she was trying to hide behind it.

"If I don't see you, Mr. Field, have a nice Thanksgiving, okay?" she said finally.

"Yeah, you too," he said, reaching out to tap her on the arm. Then Sam walked quickly away and made a beeline for the parking lot. He had to leave, and he could not bear to look Maggie in the eyes again.

Chapter 15

July 1983

They give you a small room here, in a building whose name I can never remember how to spell (a long Algonquian name) that everyone refers to simply as "The Dorm." As the summer wears on and all the counselors have gotten to know each other (maybe too well), The Dorm has also become party central. I avoid drinking too much, as I fear my stomach might be too weak, and I don't want to fall asleep in the lifeguard chair.

The other types of experimentation going on here are getting interesting.

Edna St. Vincent Millay was a pretty serious partier. She also was bisexual. "My candle burns at both ends," she wrote. "It will not last the night; but ah, my foes, and oh, my friends— It gives a lovely light."

Meg might be Edna's second coming (though I have no idea if she can write). She is spreading her light around to the luckiest boys, and she is trying to share it with me. She is a lovely girl with beautiful soft skin, and I'm sure I could enjoy the fleeting pleasure of her kisses and caresses--to the extent that I could enjoy anything. I think "fleeting" is the key word.

Oh, what a lovely light we could have made. That light has trailed off forever, like the white stream of an airplane's wake, floating above like cotton candy for a scant few minutes before it dissipates into the baby blue summer sky.

October 1983

The Saturday morning after the Walker's dance, Sam Field and Steve Morrow ran a practice, then excused the players in time for lunch. Sam was planning to go the refectory also, but first he went to his apartment to call Jackie Spellmeyer. They had met briefly a couple of days earlier at a coffee shop, where Jackie told him she was interested in his help, and they exchanged phone numbers.

Sam dialed the number from his room, and Jerry answered.

"Oh, hi, Sam, she's golfing," he said affably. "I probably won't see her until 4 or so. They don't let the ladies tee off until noon on weekends, you know."

"Oh, okay," Sam said. "Please let her know she can call me back until about 5:30, then I'm out with the kids for the evening. It's my 'master on duty' weekend, lucky me."

"Ha, good for you, I know something about how the school runs. At least you won't be subjected to a Whalers game—they're away tonight."

"Oh, I'll get the Whalers soon enough. Tonight is movie night. I'd say I'll be lucky to be in a quiet theater, except the kids won't stay quiet. They'll make their little sarcastic remarks, and then the usher will come over and scold us."

Jackie called back at 5:15. Sam explained that he had a

new piece of information from the Walker's girls, and it was about Tomas and Mallory. He also said it was a little complex, maybe even a little odd, and he wasn't sure how it would fit in with Mallory's disappearance, if at all. But he wanted to go over it with Jackie in person.

"Sure, when is good for you?"

"Well, the sooner the better. Except not tomorrow—I'm still stuck driving shuttles around. Then later this week we get into end-of-season stuff, like the awards dinner. And Thanksgiving break is right around the corner. But I have a free hour and a half early Monday or Tuesday afternoon, if either of those works for you."

"Sure, let's make it Monday. Why don't you come to my house, and we can lay out everything we know so far."

On Sunday, Sam left a few minutes early for his 5:45 student pickup, and drove a back route to Sand Hill Road so he might not be seen from Walker's. He pulled into the Cobb Montessori School parking lot and looked around. It was quiet, as he expected it would be on Sunday. There was only one car in the long lot. A man who appeared to be a maintenance worker walked out of a building carrying a green trash bag by the neck where it had been tied. He disappeared behind another building, then reappeared without the bag. As the man walked back into the original building, Sam realized it was time to drive over to Walker's.

Seven or eight Avon students piled into the van. Some had girlfriends at Walker's, others were there to hang out in groups. Walker's girls, if they were unattached, often did the same thing with groups of Avon Boys at the Old Farms campus.

Warren did not get into the van. He had already arranged with Sam for a later pickup.

A couple of hours later, Sam picked up Warren in his Capri and they drove back to Avon. Sam asked him if Annie had told him the same thing she had told Sam.

"About Tomas and Mallory and being too drunk to drive her back?"

"Yeah, well, I guess she told you. Did you ever see Mallory on those days?"

"No, Annie was in the spring play—that's how she saw her, coming out of rehearsal. I'm surprised no one else noticed anything unusual about where Mallory was walking from. Then again, Annie has three times the curiosity of most people. She sees something, or hears something, and she wants to find out more."

"Yeah, I've noticed ... Who else knows about this?"

"Just Annie, and Maggie, and me, as far as I know."

"So she told Maggie."

"Annie and Maggie tell each other everything."

Warren smiled and left it at that.

On Monday afternoon, Sam sat down at the Spellmeyers' kitchen table while Jackie made them each a cup of tea. Sam thanked her, and they both laid out their notepads.

"So, tell me about this new information," Jackie said.

"OK, but first, two questions. Obviously, you know the Walker's campus, right?"

"Yes, I've been there many times."

"What about the Cobb Montessori School just across Sand Hill Road?"

"Hmm, funny you should ask. I was just there recently. The headmistress, Reisa Maitlin, showed it to me. I was scoping out the campus, trying to imagine where he would drop her off, who else might be around, and so forth. I had an odd feeling about that Cobb school—but I digress. Go on."

"Well, the plot thickens," Sam said, leaning in. "Some Sundays, Tomas didn't drop her off. She drove herself back to campus. And since boarding students can't have cars on campus, she apparently parked in the Cobb School parking lot."

"Wait, she drove herself back? Why?"

"Sorry, I'm telling the story a little out of order. Annie told me that Tomas felt so much pressure at Avon that he sometimes drank on Sundays, the only day he didn't have classes or sports. That was also the day he would spend with Mallory, driving around, finding someplace to have sex, and so on. But he would often be woozy by late afternoon, so they had an agreement: Either one of them could decide he was too drunk to drive back, in which case she'd drop him off at home to sleep it off, and she'd drive the car back to Walker's. Well, to the Cobb School."

"Wow. Well, that does explain the empty bottle of Jack Daniel's I found in the car. And this is something Mallory told Annie?"

"Annie was in the spring play, and the theater is near Sand Hill Road. A couple of times, she said, she was leaving rehearsal when she noticed Mallory cutting across the campus from Sand Hill, and wondered why. So she confronted her about it. Mallory was reluctant at first, but she told her what was going on."

"Hmmm, you'd think maybe someone else besides Annie might have seen her."

"I wondered that too. And I mentioned it to Warren when I drove him back to Avon last night--"

"Warren was the only one in the shuttle?"

Sam laughed. "No, every now and then Warren asks me if I can pick him up later so he can spend more time with Annie."

"I hope these kids are spending enough time studying!"

"Warren is a very good student. Anyway, when I mentioned others possibly noticing Mallory's stealth walks, he pointed out that most people aren't as observant and curious as Annie. If she sees or hears something that doesn't add up, she wants to know more."

"Interesting girl. She also memorizes and catalogs a lot of information. Knows everyone's birthdays and hometowns. Then again"—here Jackie laughed at herself—"I guess I do that too."

"I just don't know what to do with this," said Sam, shaking his head. "Let's say Tomas got drunk that day, and Mallory dropped him off at his house, and then drove to the Cobb School. Was she ambushed by a stranger in the parking lot? Nobody saw her at Walker's, which is just across the road. And the authorities combed the areas around the school for evidence as soon as she was declared missing, right?"

"Yes, and they didn't find anything, but if she got forced into someone's car and driven off, there might not be much evidence left at the scene. On the other hand, not a single Walker's resident or nearby neighbor mentioned screaming, strange men or vehicles cruising the area, or anything like that."

"What about Tomas and his family," Sam asked. "Have you questioned them?

"Tomas briefly after one of his summer baseball games, and his father Mario one Saturday morning in September. Tomas stuck to his story about dropping her off at Walker's. We now know that might not be true, but something tells me Tomas wouldn't want to talk about the drinking."

"And Mario? If Tomas was drunk, there are at least three people who might have seen him stagger into the house."

"Mario said he was cooking at his restaurant job that evening, and that he thinks Tomas was sleeping when he got home. I have not talked to Anna or Nico. I don't know what kind of Sunday dinner routine they have. Tomas was living like an 18-year-old kid with a busy schedule, a girlfriend and a car. Parents sometimes lose track. And generally, if any given day seems ordinary when it's happening, people have a really hard time remembering details when you ask them about it five months later."

"So, you have seen the car?"

"Yes, but I'd like to see it again. I didn't get a chance to look as carefully as I would have liked. Mario was getting restless for me to leave."

Sam was thinking about what the detective Thomas Fenton had told him about searching cars.

"Well," Sam said, "I've got one more class to teach this

afternoon. We are missing a clue or two, that's for sure. With this new information, do you think you'll try to talk to Tomas and Mario again? It's weird for me, I see Nico every day. He has no idea I'm talking to you. And any way you look at it, Tomas is still part of this case."

"Yeah, you know, my gut instinct is still that Tomas and Mario are basically decent people. But my other gut instinct—and this comes from decades of doing this—tells me they are not telling everything they know. Well, it *was* a gut instinct. Now we know they aren't."

The next couple of weeks passed in a blur for Sam, who had final term assignments to give out, tests to grade, and soccer awards to create, individually tailored to his players. He also dusted off his skates and got out on the rink a couple of times to get his skating legs back and get ready for his winter sports assignment as assistant coach of thirds hockey.

Jackie spent most of that time puzzling over the information she had, checking in with Reisa, writing out possible scenarios on her flow charts, and considering a trip to Storrs after Thanksgiving. She didn't want to disrupt the Arpantes' holiday, and she had her own houseful of relatives descending on Simsbury. She did make her scheduled check-in call to the Hardings, but did not reveal the new information because she still didn't know what to make of it, and didn't want to upset Mallory's parents with a new hornet's nest of what-ifs.

Sam and Jackie met one more time before break to discuss, and mostly dismiss, other possible suspects. George Dickleman had a long rap sheet of sexual indiscretions with mothers of his students, but his extracurricular activities seemed to begin and end there. Juan Ortega displayed an outward interest in people's sex lives generally, and threw the f-word around like a Frisbee, but seemed content to leave it at that. He lived with his wife and young son in a house near the campus, and the only speculation that ever got whispered around campus was that he might have slept with fellow Cuban teacher Merriam Rodriguez, but no one cared to confirm it. And in spite of his exhorting Sam and Joe to ask the Walker's girls to dance, he did no such thing himself.

With no obvious suspects (besides Tomas) among the Avon students and faculty, Jackie had spent a couple of hours going through lists of Walker's faculty and staff with Reisa Maitlin, but she could not same a single one who had ever raised suspicions, and they had all sailed through their background checks. A stable hand who had a murky background was not hired—and that was at least three or four years ago, Reisa said. Jackie had also gone over assaults and other possible sex crimes in the town of Simsbury with Brad Sullivan, which did not turn up anyone suspicious as related to Mallory's case.

The only new wrinkle in the case, suspect-wise, had come with the knowledge that Mallory and Tomas had been using the Cobb Montessori School parking lot for dropping off and picking up the Riviera when Tomas was too drunk to drive. Sam mentioned the maintenance worker he had observed there on Sunday. Sam said he did not get a suspicious vibe from the man—and that he was clearly taking care of business, not scoping the area for teenage girls—but Jackie said she'd meet with administrators there to make sure there were no stones unturned.

As Sam was leaving the Spellmeyer home, he had a sudden thought.

"Oh wait," he said. "There is someone—"

"Yes?" Jackie asked as he paused.

"This is weird. Seems pretty farfetched. But it's the only person I've ever heard speak ill of Mallory Harding."

Sam related the story of his odd encounter at O'Laughlin's with a drunken Victoria Lavelle, and how she said Mallory "had it coming to her."

"That is weird," agreed Jackie. "And you say she spoke to a Walker's assembly, and that she works for the state when she's not knocking back Manhattans at the bar?"

"Yeah, but I have no idea what department."

"Probably some sort of counseling division within the state ed department. Reisa will know. And I guess I'll have to pay Miss Lavelle a visit."

Avon gave a full week off for Thanksgiving break, so classes ended Friday and the campus basically shut down on Saturday. Friday night, Sam, Joe Grisman, Steve Morrow, and Mark Lehrer made plans to go out. They talked about driving into downtown Hartford, where the bars were livelier and the possibilities for chatting up single women were exponentially greater.

Sam, Joe and Mark would be packing for a trip "home" the next day. All in their early 20s, they treated their Avon gig almost as an extension of college, and still decamped to their family's homes in the Northeast for holidays. Steve, at 30, did not have close family in the area, and his Avon apartment was his home until he moved on to his next prep school job somewhere else. Other faculty who lived on or near campus full-time made sure that any single teachers who stuck around received a Thanksgiving dinner invitation.

That night, the young bachelors decided to stay close, and started with a beer at a pub on 44 where a folksinger was playing. Then they moved on to O'Laughlin's, where a boisterous Friday night crowd was yakking it up over Irish music on the jukebox while Kieran held forth at the bar, his brogue reaching new heights of absurdity--or so Sam thought.

"I'm telling you, he's from Iowa," he joked to his friends.

The men shared a couple of pitchers and talked about the usual subjects--their students, their classes and sports, and the eccentricities of the headmaster and the other faculty. Joe brought up the dance at Walker's and how Juan had urged them to ask the girls to dance, saying they were "ripe like summertime fruit."

"Why aren't you out there dancing with them?" Joe said, imitating Juan's deep, gravelly voice.

"More like, 'Why aren't you outside fucking them?'," added Steve as the others broke into laughter.

"I don't know, though," said Joe, "Sam here seems to be on a first-name basis with a bunch of Walker's girls. What you got goin' on, big guy?"

"Save me some leftovers," snorted Mark.

"Come on guys," Sam said. "Warren's on my hall, and he's become my buddy. So he introduced me to his girlfriend and a few of their friends. No big deal. Nothing to see here."

"Although," Sam added with a wink and an elbow to Joe's side, "Can I help it if they all think I'm hot?"

After the hoots subsided, Sam excused himself to go to the men's room. When he emerged, he took a couple of steps and then froze. He realized that the last time he had been here, the poster of Mallory was just over his left shoulder from where he was standing. He wasn't sure he wanted to turn around and look. At that moment, he thought he heard a woman somewhere in the bar say, "We haven't had enough rain lately. Hopefully we'll get more soon."

Sam looked around to see who had made that comment; the only conversations near him that he could overhear were not about the weather. And with the steady general hum of relatively loud voices going on, he was not sure why his ears had picked up that comment. Finally, he turned and looked at the wall, and there she was—Mallory, still staring directly at him, still with the same haunting expression. Suddenly, his ears went blank to the din of the crowd, and he thought he heard a faint voice whispering in his head: *Don't stop now. You're getting closer.*

Stunned, Sam waited for more, but the spaces in his head filled up with bar noise again. He fought off a chill, and went back to the table.

Later that night as he turned the key to his apartment, Sam was lost in thought about Mallory. His reverie was interrupted when he noticed the light blinking on his answering machine. He pressed the play button, and was surprised at the voice he heard. She had never called him on the phone before.

"Hi Mr. Field, it's Maggie. Maggie Duchesne. I'm leaving for New York tomorrow. I think I may have said this that night at Walker's, but I would like to wish you a happy Thanksgiving. That's all. Talk to you soon."

Sam took a deep breath, walked over to his bed, removed his shoes and pants, and flung himself backward onto the mattress, where he stared at the ceiling until sleep overtook him.

Chapter 16

July 1983

Not so long ago, I felt that my life was opening up before me like a flower in springtime, that a world of new experiences was waiting for me to take it on if only I dared. I was shy, but your confidence made me more daring.

I savored those days, and my heart felt full with possibility. And love. More than romantic or sexual love--big, infinite love. Love that filled me up and warmed my soul like a June sun in a cloudless sky.

Love comes cheap these days. It's not all that it wants to be or that I want it to be. In truth, it isn't really love at all. It's a game we play to see if our blood is flowing and our nerve endings are functioning properly. Our lips moisten, our bodies tremble in anticipation, and our skin receives and reacts to impulses from the touch of another. But the delirious, fleeting sensations don't find their way to my heart.

"I had to trust life," wrote Maya Angelou, "since I was young enough to believe that life loved the person who dared to live it."

Once I was young enough to trust life too. I dared and I

lived. Now I don't trust anything or anyone, and I can't get the clouds to stop blocking the sun.

November 1983

Sam drove northward on I-91 on a crisp, dry, and cool mid-November day. He reflected on his first two and a half months of teaching at Avon. It had been a whirlwind of new people and new experiences: learning to teach history and prepare lesson plans, grading papers, dealing with teenage boys who could be wayward, sarcastic, and unpredictable, but who also seemed to warm up to Sam and appreciate his guidance. He loved coaching the soccer team, and he found that he didn't mind monitoring study hall or taking the boys on weekend activities.

Sam did not have a girlfriend and had not had much of a social life beyond beers with the other single teachers. As for a love life, the few passing flirtations with women in bars had not amounted to anything. And the one momentary thrill—his kiss with Maggie—was not something to be celebrated or repeated. He was looking forward to downtime at his parents' house in Northampton, idle afternoons reading in coffeeshops, beers with his high school buddies at Packard's, a house full of relatives who would come in for Thanksgiving dinner, and a pizza date on Friday evening with his ex-girlfriend Katie.

As a child, Sam had been fascinated by the Connecticut River whenever he could see it from his parents' car, either when they crossed the Calvin Coolidge Bridge on their way to

Amherst to watch a college football game or buy pumpkins at Atkins Farms, or when they drove down I-91 to New Haven or Hammonasset Beach on Long Island Sound. Interstate 91 ran mostly to the west of the river; it crossed over from west to east at Windsor Locks, and back again at Chicopee. He loved looking down at what seemed to him to be the widest and mightiest river in the world, and imagining himself navigating it on a raft, like Huck Finn. And it filled him with wonder during seasons of heavy rain, when the river would spill out onto flood plains, and the trees appeared to be growing straight out of the water.

On this drive home for Thanksgiving, he observed the opposite extreme. The river seemed unusually low, with exposed riverbeds on either side. He occasionally saw boats still tied to their docks but sitting partly up on mud and sand. He knew there had not been much rain this autumn, but he was surprised at how dry the river looked.

He remembered the woman's voice he heard in the bar the previous night, complaining that there hadn't been enough rain. He never saw who made the remark, and he was puzzled that his ears had singled it out from the other noise in the bar.

After Sam lugged his duffel into his old bedroom and tossed it onto the bed, he came back out to the kitchen and described to his parents what the Connecticut River had looked like.

"Yeah, everyone's complaining about the lack of rain," his father said. "But the forecast looks better--I should say wetter--for later in the week. Two storm systems merging in the Ohio Valley and then heading our way. Hopefully we'll get a good soaking."

Sam smiled at his father's lifelong obsession with, and tracking of, the weather.

For the next few days, Sam enjoyed the peacefulness of being home with no pressing work to do and no rowdy teenagers to tend to. He slept late, took walks, enjoyed his mother's cooking, and watched TV with his parents in the evenings. He walked into town to browse the merchandise at Main Street Records, the Globe Bookstore, and the shops at Thornes Marketplace. He chatted with old acquaintances in the streets, and spent hours drinking coffee and reading in the local cafes. The particulars of the Mallory Harding case drifted into the background while he recharged, and he had pretty much decided not to bring it up with his family and friends.

Party night finally arrived, and on Wednesday evening, Sam met up with several old friends who were in town for the holiday. There were the engineers: Tom, who worked for a chemical company in Buffalo; Jordy, employed by a tech startup on Route 128 outside Boston; and Dave, an aerospace engineer yearning to be a full-time artist, who had just flown in from Los Angeles, where he worked for General Dynamics. Only Tony, after four years at Middlebury College, had settled again in Northampton to work in his father's carpet business. "Just for a year," he had told his friends at first. "I'm not going to take the business over." It was now two-plus years and counting.

They began the reunion at Fitzwilly's, an upscale "fern

bar" frequented by professionals, academics, and students who were at least 20 or could pass for it. It also was a favorite among lesbians and gays, who thrived in this notoriously progressive and welcoming city. And at 9 o'clock, the hum of conversation was modest enough that the old friends could share their more in-depth stories that were best told without constant interruption by partiers who no longer could tell how loudly they were shouting.

Dave, who told his friends he moved to California to be "on the other side of the Rockies from my parents," said he mostly enjoyed his work and his coworkers, but that he was so determined to become a graphic artist for a film company that he had personally visited several of them with two envelopes full of samples—one to leave with the receptionist for the person in charge of design, and one to hand to an unsuspecting employee with no direction to deliver them to anyone in particular.

The others talked about the cities they lived in, and their latest encounters with women. No one was married, and only Tony had a steady girlfriend. And besides Dave, no one else had much to say about their work, but they were interested in Sam's--*What's it like? Are they all rich spoiled brats? Are there any girls' schools around? Do you catch the boys masturbating?*

"Ha, no, not masturbating. And I haven't caught any of them drinking yet. I have to be careful who I report anyway, because any given kid, the headmaster might be banging his mother."

"Really? Is that a condition of being admitted to the school?" asked Jordy.

"Well, in a few cases, it may be. George keeps a secret apartment off-campus. If one of the moms strikes his fancy, he goes in for the kill. I don't think he sleeps with his own wife."

"Ah, the secret sex lives of the private boys' school," laughed Tom. "You should write a book. What about you? You getting' it on with the French teacher? Or maybe a pretty young heiress from a nearby girls' school?"

"Hmm, well there is a senior at Ethel Walker's who has a wicked crush on me," said Sam before deciding to change the subject. "But no, no action to speak of. Most of the female teachers are married. Only the French teacher is single—funny you said that. Not my type, though. Miss Frelet. The kids call her 'Free Lay.' Anyway, the local bars aren't exactly teeming with prospects. You have to go into Hartford for that, and, well, nothing promising so far. But speaking of promising, those two ladies at the bar might be checking us out."

"Probably a couple of lesbos trying to determine how Neanderthal we are," said Jordy.

"Really?" Sam replied in a scolding tone, turning to Jordy. "*Lesbos?* C'mon, Northampton might be the most gay-friendly city in the country, and you grew up here, and that's how you--"

"I'd say Provincetown is the most gay-friendly city in the country," interjected Dave.

"Are you serious? Provincetown is not a city," countered Sam. "It's a tiny little resort town with one street."

"Well, they pack a lot of gays and *les-bee-ans* into that one street for the transvestite parades," said Jordy. "And by the way, I was kidding."

"OK then," said Dave, "San Francisco is the most gay-friendly city in the country."

"That's because all the hippies are too stoned to remember to be prejudiced," joked Tom. "Oh, and by the way, Buffalo's a pretty gay-friendly place too, which not a lot of outsiders realize. You know, old industrial town. Seems counter-intuitive."

"Anyway, since you brought it up, let's try a little experiment," said Sam. "Are we having one more here? You guys can order from the waitress. I'll go up to the bar and order a beer there, right next to Gertrude and Alice. And I'll let you know just how castrating they are."

"Go for it, Casanova," said Tony.

Sam never bragged about his pick-up skills. In fact, he had grown up feeling insecure about his attractiveness. But his male friends saw him differently, and some of them seemed mildly jealous that Sam was often the one who attracted attention. When they pointed that out to him, he would tell them that it's a game of percentages. Play enough times and you win one here and there.

The four friends sat and watched Sam work his magic—slowly at first, until he and the two women were all laughing, talking animatedly, and occasionally touching each other's arm or shoulder.

"Damn him," said Jordy. "He does that thing where he starts of slow and shy, with a self-effacing remark or two, then next thing you know they're pawing him."

After 20 minutes, Sam returned to the table. "They're

going to Packard's," he announced, grinning. "Which, if memory serves, is where we said we would end up tonight."

The group spent a couple of hours at Packard's, playing pool and darts, drinking more beer, and ordering bar food to soak it up. Sam introduced his new friends to his old ones. They drifted through the evening, breaking into smaller groups and pairs as they continued the increasingly tipsy conversations. Other high school friends mingled in. As closing time neared, the two women from Fitzwilly's had separated; one of them, named Mary, stayed close to Sam.

Tom caught up with Sam in the men's room. He mentioned that they were making plans to get together on Friday night with a couple of other classmates who were home.

"Ah, sounds like fun," said Sam. "But I have a date."

"With the girl from Fitzwilly's?" asked Tom. "You dirty dog."

"No, actually, Katie."

"Oh, I see," said Tom, smiling. "You just can't let that go, can you."

"We're friends now," said Sam. "Good friends."

"Uh-huh."

"I mean it."

"Well, anyway," said Tom, "we're going to go over to the Red Lion Diner after this for a late breakfast. You in?"

"Well, actually, I have plans after this too--"

Tom looked puzzled for a second until he realized what was going on, then burst into a laugh. "You have a great time tonight, OK?"

"Maybe I'll catch you before we head back," said Sam. "A

skate on Friday afternoon, a drink on Saturday, something like that. I'll call you."

As they left the men's room, they saw Mary a few yards away. Sam turned to face Tom so Mary couldn't hear what he said.

"It's been a dry fall, but I guess it's my lucky week."

The next day, although Sam was tired from a long night out, he enjoyed Thanksgiving dinner with family and relatives, and the tradition of talking well into the evening with wine still on the table. He went to bed relatively early, and felt more refreshed on Friday. Rather than drive to Amherst or Holyoke for a skate, Sam and a few friends decided to walk and window shop in downtown Northampton. When Sam got home, there was a message to call Katie.

Hearing her voice on the other end of the line felt like snuggling into a big comfy sweatshirt. She confirmed she was still on for the night; pizza at Joe's, then whatever else they decided. Sam offered to pick her up, but Katie said, "That's OK, I can take my mother's Bonneville. I'll get you at 7."

Sam hung up and sighed. Already, he was having an involuntary physical reaction to the fact that Katie had made it clear what direction the evening would take. They were both staying in family homes crowded with extra visitors. His Mercury Capri had bucket seats separated by the stick shift. Her mother's Pontiac Bonneville had such a wide front seat that it probably could seat four people across, except that it was not legal to do so.

Sam Field and Katie Trimble had been high school sweethearts, but after a few too many fights, they had agreed to break up and move on soon after graduation. Still, somehow, they kept circling back to each other. As their on-again, off-again relationship mellowed into their college and young working years, two things remained constant: They never tired of each other sexually, and the affinity they shared for each other never wavered. They were just as comfortable getting together after a long separation as they were a short one.

As they left Joe's, a light rain had begun to fall. Katie suggested picking up a six-pack at State Street Fruit. Few words were necessary as Katie drove toward Florence. She placed her right hand on Sam's thigh, and he placed a hand over hers. The rain grew steadier. She parked at their old favorite secluded spot at the edge of Look Park.

"You sure we won't get stuck in the mud?" Sam asked.

"There's no mud yet," Katie laughed.

They talked and drank one beer each, and then Katie pulled off her sweater. The rain sounded cold and menacing as it plunked steadily on the roof of the Bonneville, but inside, the car was warm. Soon it felt even warmer as they wrapped each other up in the old familiar clutch. Their steady rhythm was slow and sensual compared to the insistently pelting rain. They buried their faces in each others' bodies until waves of release finally overtook them. They grew still, savoring the moment, holding each other tightly, listening to the rain. Sam noticed a single tear running down Katie's cheek, and wiped it off with his finger.

"Don't worry, I'm OK," she whispered. "After all we've been through, sometimes I forget how happy you make me."

"Yeah, me too," said Sam.

Presently they sat up straight again and opened two more beers. Katie talked about her jobs in Boston: some low-paying work for a film company she hoped would lead to bigger opportunities, and waitress jobs to pay the bills. Sam talked about his teaching, and coaching, and the raucous kids, then strayed into a topic he had left alone all week. He told her about the disappearance of an Ethel Walker School student named Mallory Harding, and how, thanks to his coincidental contacts with Mallory's friends, he had been enlisted by a local private investigator to help with the case.

He told her about the boyfriend she had spent the day with. Most people, he said, had assumed foul play, either by Tomas or some other man who kidnapped her. But so far there was no evidence to make anything stick, and the few details they did know about the car, where they might have spent the afternoon, and what Mallory's friends had told Sam about Tomas' drinking only raised more questions than they answered.

Sam also told Katie about the posters of Mallory he had seen in town, and how they always gave him an eerie feeling that she was watching him, maybe even trying to communicate with him—so much so that on a couple of occasions, he could have sworn he heard a voice inside his head, pleading with him to keep looking.

"Well," said Katie, "that's a lot to digest. I have a couple of thoughts. First, have the police, or you and your P.I., considered any other potential suspects?"

"Umm ..." he stammered in response. Sam had been wondering of late if they should cast a wider net. "Not very many," he admitted. "We threw names around. The Avon headmaster has wandering eyes, but seems fixated on older mothers, not teenage girls. The Walker's headmistress did not know of any male teachers or employees who had had suspicious interactions with Mallory. And I asked a couple of Mallory's best friends if they thought any Avon boys might be obsessed with her, and came up empty. The last boyfriend she had committed suicide, but not over Mallory—"

"Really!" exclaimed Katie. "And how do you know it wasn't over Mallory?"

"He was gay. And he couldn't admit it—not to anyone at Avon, not to his mother, not to himself. He had a hundred issues pent up inside him. But--a story for another time."

"So," Katie said, shifting her position as she readied her thoughts on Sam's mystical experiences with the poster. "I get that when a girl goes missing, first you look at the men in her life. The boyfriend or ex-husband or abusive father. Then you look for other men who might have been obsessed with her. By the way, was she pretty? Maybe more importantly, was she charismatic?"

"Well, I never got to meet her, but by all accounts, yes and yes."

"And you said that, through your buddy Warren on your hall, you've met something like six of Mallory's closest friends?"

"Yes—why?"

"OK, I don't know whether I believe in supernatural forces or not. I go back and forth. But tonight I'll be a believer. And I've known you for so long—"

With that, Katie broke off her sentence and looked Sam hard in his eyes. She leaned over and pressed her lips into his for a long second, then resumed talking.

"I've known you for so long that I don't think you'd make this up. Now maybe it's some kind of delirious response you're having whenever you see her face and wonder where she possibly could have gone. But I don't think so. I do think that Mallory is trying to communicate with you because she knows that you—not the police, not the P.I.—have access to those girls and the inner workings of their group. And that's where—somewhere within that group—I think you might start to find answers."

"Wait. You don't think maybe—"

"I do think maybe," she said, gazing into his eyes again. "And by the way, whatever you do find that seems suspicious, or sounds like someone's trying to hide something, don't ever underestimate what a girl might be capable of."

"Oh, Jesus, Katie," Sam said, wrapping his arms around her.

The rain was still pelting furiously against the roof of the Bonneville. Sam and Katie had one more beer to drink, and one more hour to share in each other's comforting arms before they would leave each other again until God knows when.

At five o'clock on Saturday, the phone rang at the Field house. "Sam, it's for you," his mother called out. Jackie Spellmeyer had tracked down the number.

"When are you coming back?" she asked.

"Monday, I guess. Classes start Tuesday. Smart thing Avon does so no one has to travel on the busiest—"

"You might want to consider coming back tomorrow. But that's your call. They found her. A jogger saw what looked like remains in the Farmington River from the bridge on 44. Police suspect the heavy rain dislodged her from somewhere upriver. The identification has not been made official, but the inside word is it's her."

Chapter 17

July 1983

What if I could just throw out the past and move on to the next stage of my life, blissfully ignorant of where I was and what I did the year before—better yet, all the years before?

Zelda Fitzgerald compared it to emptying an ashtray. "I just lump everything in a great heap which I have labeled 'the past,' and having thus emptied this deep reservoir that was once myself, I am ready to continue."

Easier said than done—even for her, I should think. Unless she was on massive medication. We can't chase away our demons simply by pretending to forget they ever were there. What thinking person can forget what it was like to love, to yearn, to feel excitement, to experience rejection? To be hurt so badly that you want to hurt back harder?

The pain ebbs but leaves behind an aching heart. The bleeding stops but leaves a scar. And the emptiness inside you isn't just a blank space—it's a blank space with jagged edges. It's a blank space you can feel cutting into your soul. It's infinitely bigger and more powerful than a pile of stale cigarette butts, and you can't just dump it out and be done with it.

November 1983

Sam sought out Juan Ortega and found him in the quad talking with Kevin. Several boys had collected around Kevin's door, but the men were speaking to each other in hushed tones several yards away. Juan turned to Sam.

"You heard the news, right?"

"Possibly before you did," Sam replied.

Juan cast Sam a look of measured skepticism. He had heard rumors—mostly through Kevin's pipeline—that Sam had gotten to know several of Mallory's friends at Walker's, and that his connections had earned him a hush-hush agreement to assist the P.I. on the case, Jackie Spellmeyer. Juan wouldn't have minded except that he prided himself on knowing more about the school and its secrets than most of the teachers.

"Based on where the body was found," said Kevin, "It points more toward foul play close to the Avon campus as opposed to Walker's. I'm afraid they're going to take another hard look at Tomas."

"How do you figure?" said Sam, puzzled. "She was found under the bridge on 44. It's likely the remains floated down from somewhere upriver, which puts her closer to the town of Simsbury, and to the Walker's campus."

Juan smiled, then let out a hearty laugh. "You young teachers, you think you know it all."

Sam cocked his head, not sure what Juan was getting at.

Juan sighed, crossed his arms, and began his master class.

"The Mississippi River flows north to south," he began, "from northern Minnesota to the Gulf of Mexico."

After a slight pause for effect, he continued. "The Hudson River flows north to south, from the Adirondack mountains to New York Harbor and the Atlantic Ocean. Our own Connecticut River flows north to south, from Fourth Connecticut Lake in Pittsburg, New Hampshire, rolling past us about seven miles east of where we're standing, and on into Long Island Sound."

Juan smiled at Sam again, and continued his geography lesson.

"So, given that preponderance of evidence, I suppose you can be forgiven for assuming all rivers flow north to south. But that's not always the case. Not with the Red River, which flows northward between Minnesota and North Dakota and on up into Manitoba. And not with the Deschutes and Willamette rivers in Oregon, which both flow northward into the Columbia River."

"OK," Sam said, smiling and crossing his arms as he began rethinking his conclusions. "So you're telling me the Farmington River also flows south to north."

"Well, it's not quite that simple," Juan said, clearly having a good time being the all-knowing geography geek. "Two branches of the Farmington form in southwestern Massachusetts, flowing southward into Connecticut until they join in New Hartford. Then the river flows southeastward until it reaches the town of Farmington, then turns and flows due north through Avon and Simsbury. Finally, it snakes its way east-southeast to Windsor, just south of Bradley Field, where it spills into the Connecticut. That's right where Loomis Chafee School is, by the way."

"So it flows right near our athletic fields, doesn't it," said Sam. "Northward, passing under 44, what, about two miles downriver?"

"That's right. Maybe 500 yards from our fields. Remember that park you asked me about?"

"Yeah, Fisher Meadows. You told me that's where teenagers go to make out."

"Haha, I'm sure that's not how I put it."

"Yeah," Sam agreed, "I'm sure it isn't."

"Good place to dump a body," Kevin said. "At least, that's what my kids think."

"Do your kids think they know who might have done it?" Sam asked. "Do they think it was Tomas after all?"

Kevin paused and moved another step away from his door, where two students were still talking. "Who knows what they think," he said finally. "On other topics, they tell me a lot. But other than the comment about dumping a body, they've been mostly quiet on this. I don't think anyone wants to associate Tomas with Mallory's death, or even say his name out loud. Some of them were good friends. And he is an Avon legend of sorts."

"Is that it then?" said Sam. "No other info or leads from them?"

"Nah, I don't think so," Kevin said.

Juan excused himself and strode away toward his next class. Kevin turned toward the teenagers and said, "Almost class time, guys."

Turning back to Sam, he said, "Unless …"

"Unless what?"

"Nah, I don't see what …"

"OK Kevin, let's have it."

"I think at least one of my kids mentioned he was down at the soccer fields that day with a group of students. Surprised he even remembered. But he didn't say anything else about it. No one said they saw something, or heard anything coming from Fisher Meadows."

"Oh? They go down to the fields on Sunday? What do they do there? Kick the soccer ball around? Toss a football? Frisbee?"

Kevin smiled. "Maybe. But that's not the main reason they're there. Some Walker's girls who don't have steady boyfriends come to our fields on Sundays to hang out with Avon boys who don't have girlfriends. Sometimes they have their eye on someone. Sometimes they're just trying to make an impression to see if one of the boys or girls thinks they're cute or funny. Reese cracks them up, but the girls don't see him as a prospect, if you know what I mean. One of my kids, Jimmy Harper, goes down there sometimes. Great kid, good looking if he gave it any effort, but shy. He's been asking me for tips on how to talk to girls."

"Do you think he'd talk to me?"

"Well, you already know Reese—and he's not shy!"

"Oh, yeah, that's true."

While waiting for the medical examiner's report, Jackie Spellmeyer was formulating a plan. With the new information she had from Sam via Annie Green, she wanted to confront

Tomas again, this time at UConn. But first she wanted to do a more though search of the Buick Riviera. As a P.I., she could not secure a warrant herself. She considered asking Brad Sullivan, but decided instead to call in a favor from an old colleague in the West Hartford P.D.

A few days later, Lieutenant Brady Stimpson had secured a warrant. He and Jackie, along with Hartford County Sheriff Don Masterson, planned to execute the warrant that Friday morning at the Arpante home. Nico would not be there because of school; they did not know Mario's and Anna's schedules, but hoped they would catch one of them at home. Sam was teaching anyway, but was advised to stay away.

Sam told Jackie he understood. But he also reminded her what Thomas Fenton had told him. Look under all the seats. Look down into the spaces between the seat cushions where seatbelts disappear. "You'd be surprised how deep those crevices can be, especially in the older American cars," Sam told her.

"No, Sam, I wouldn't be surprised," she said, smiling.

On Friday morning, Sheriff Masterson drove to the Arpante home with Lieutenant Stimpson and Jackie Spellmeyer and parked in the driveway. A living room curtain parted briefly. Masterson rang the doorbell and knocked three times on the door. At first, all was quiet inside.

He knocked again.

Finally, the door creaked open. "What is it this time?" crowed Mario Arpante, clearly angry and frustrated. "Haven't you harassed this family enough?"

Don held up the warrant, and Jackie stepped forward.

"Mr. Arpante, I know that this has been an ordeal for you and your family. I am sorry to have to bother you again. But I'm sure you are aware that they found the girl's remains last weekend."

"Yes, under Route 44 a good two miles upriver from the Avon campus. And god knows how far the body floated, with all that rain. Someone must have dumped it way up in Simsbury, probably after abducting her from Walker's."

"Actually, Mr. Arpante, the 44 bridge is downriver from the Avon campus," corrected Lieutenant Stimpson. "The Farmington River flows northward from the town of Farmington through Avon and Simsbury. So we consider it likely that her body was disposed of in the river somewhere in the general vicinity of Avon."

Mario was silent for a moment, having lost the geography argument.

"So what more do you want, then," Mario said. "I've answered all of your questions."

"We have a warrant to search Tomas' car," Jackie said. "Mallory Harding was last seen in that car with him. So there's no getting around that we need to do it. I don't know what we'll find, if anything. Is it in the garage, and may we have the keys?"

The three of them carefully examined the Riviera's trunk, which contained mostly sports equipment and a couple of blankets. Under the seats, they found candy wrappers, empty water and soda bottles, two empty 375-ml bottles of Jack Daniel's, loose change, a condom wrapper, a hairbrush, and a half-full plastic box of white Tic Tac mints.

Jackie took photographs of several dents on the car.

Jackie then dug into the gaps between the seat and upright sections of the upholstery. In the backseat, she found two more condom wrappers and more loose change. There was nothing of note in the driver's side seat, but what she found on the passenger side intrigued her the most. It looked like the contents of a woman's handbag, including lipstick, concealer, a pen, an earring, and what appeared to be a pocket-sized journal.

The investigators collected the items of interest and placed them in a large plastic bag. Mario was told that they would be kept for at the sheriff's headquarters until all parties considered their inspections to be complete. At such point, said Sheriff Masterson, the items would be returned to the Arpante household. Mario said nothing, offering only a blank stare that seemed to say, "What would I want with them?"

At the sheriff's office, Jackie examined the items one by one, taking notes, especially as she flipped through the pages of the journal. When she got home, she called Sam and left him a message.

When Sam got back from class, he played back his message and called Jackie.

"OK, so Fenton was right," she began. "Lots of stuff can fall down those spaces. I bet he catches cheaters that way, examining the seats where they've had sex."

"Ha, you're probably right," said Sam. "And I bet he just breaks into the car without a warrant."

"Knowing him, it wouldn't surprise me," she said. "Now, I'm going to need your connections at Walker's. One of the most interesting things I found on the passenger side was a pocket-size journal, presumably Mallory's. There were only eight entries in it, before it stopped—which would make sense, if that's when she stopped."

"Did it look like a girl's handwriting?" he asked.

"Well, I don't like to make assumptions--"

"You can tell."

"Yes," she sighed, "usually you can tell—unless it's my mother. But yes, it has the characteristics of a young girl's handwriting. And it gets interesting."

"How so?"

"Well, at first, it's all sunshine and birds singing. "I can't wait to see you today," "Being near you warms my soul," that sort of thing.

"But about halfway through," she continued, "It takes a funny turn. Like something has gone awry with the relation-ship. Unless--"

"Unless what?" Sam asked.

There was a brief silence while Jackie thought through a second possibility.

"OK, what I need you to do is try to find out if Tomas was breaking up with her. And if not that ..."

"Yes?"

"This seems farfetched, but could she have fallen in love with a different guy, a guy she would have left Tomas for—except he rejected her advances?"

"Wow," Sam said. "Neither of those scenarios sounds like anything Annie or Maggie shared with me. But I can ask them. I was also thinking that Mallory's other friends might be worth talking to."

Sam had not yet shared with Jackie the nature of his conversation with Katie about the other girls in the circle.

"Sure," Jackie said. "I think that's a good idea. You might want to start with Mallory's roommate, the Fiorini girl."

"Now what did you read in that journal that made you think there was trouble brewing in their relationship?"

"About halfway in, the writing—which is very good, by the way--begins to take on a more mournful tone. Wistful talk about rejection and hurt. And quotes from famous female writers, like Charlotte Bronte, who wrote, "Out of the fullness of the heart, the mouth speaketh and truly I find it difficult to be cheerful so long as I think I shall never see you more.""

"Do you have the journal in front of you?"

"No, I can't bring it home. It's at the sheriff's office. But I took notes. Here's another one, from Emily Dickinson: "Parting is all we need to know of hell.""

"Did you take down anything that seems to be in Mallory's own voice?"

A couple of them. Here's one:

"My soul reached out to touch yours, and we almost connected. It seemed to me the stars shone more brightly that night than they ever had before. Their celestial energy lit my heart on fire, and I thought yours might catch too. And maybe it did, but only for a moment. Then the light flickered and went dim, as if someone had thrown a veil over the heavens. And I could feel you pushing me away, like the dawn pushing the night away over the western horizon."

"Wow," said Sam. "That's pretty vivid imagery. And emotional too. Somebody's heart was breaking."

"Somebody's?"

"Well," he said. "That could very well be from Mallory's journal."

He paused, trying to grasp the feeling that was coming over him. Then he spoke.

"But what if it isn't?"

Chapter 18

August 1983

I wonder sometimes if I have the courage to confront what lies ahead of me.

I have found courage in the past. When I had nothing, and no one had my back, I reached deep within me and came up with courage, with a will to press forward and become someone I wanted to be. Someone I was meant to be. Someone others could admire, and dare I say it, love.

But I fear that the courage I once found has left me. It visited for a season and now is gone. It snuck out the window while I slept. It took the five-forty-eight and missed its stop. It stepped out to buy a pack of cigarettes and kept going. My fickle courage is having a smoke somewhere else, sitting on a dock in a different country, overlooking a different ocean.

Alice Mackenzie Swaim said this: "Courage is not the towering oak that sees storms come and go. It is the fragile blossom that opens in the snow."

I'd like to be that fragile blossom. But I believe my soul now is in perpetual winter. I am the fragile blossom that opens in the snow, then keels over.

December 1983

On Monday morning, both Jackie and Sam had appointments to set up. Jackie called an acquaintance in the University of Connecticut registrar's office who had helped her in the past when she needed to reach someone on the campus. She explained the situation briefly and asked for Tomas' class schedule and the best way to get a message to him without calling his dorm room, which she did not want to do. She hadn't decided yet whether to drive directly to Storrs or try to get him on a private call first, in which case she would reveal the new information she had, and try to convince him to give her a new statement before the police found out.

Sam waited for Warren to emerge from his dorm room on his way to his first class; as they walked across the quad, Sam asked if Warren could set up a meeting in town—maybe a pizza night—with Annie, Maggie, and Suzanne Fiorini. With the new information he had, it was time to ask the girls a few more questions, and to bring Mallory's former roommate into the mix.

Sam didn't know Reese's schedule, but assumed he would run into him in the quad or at lunch. Sure enough, when Sam walked into the refectory, Reese was already seated. Sam tapped him on the shoulder and asked him if he wouldn't mind chatting with him for a few minutes after lunch.

"Does it matter if I mind or not?" Reese asked.

"Well, no, I guess it doesn't," Sam said. "See you outside."

Reese came out and walked up to Sam. "What's up, Mr. Field? Looking for some advice on how to pick up girls?"

"Ah, well, at my age we call them women, but any advice you've got, I'm all ears."

"Oh, silly me, I thought you preferred the young ones. Anyway, what's up?"

"Great soccer season, by the way," Sam said. "I had fun—I hope you did. And thanks for all the help. It's easier to coach when you know someone else is chasing all the balls that went flying into the woods."

"Ten bucks says there's still a few balls in those woods. I'm not that diligent, especially if there's a dry seat at the end of the bench with my ass's name on it. But that's not why you asked to see me."

"Well, speaking of the soccer fields, I hear you and some friends hang out down there on Sundays."

"If you're trying to get me to rat out someone for smoking, you might just as well ask Mr. Dickleman which mom he's banging this week."

"No, no, I wouldn't put you in that position. Not today, anyway. But I would like to draw on your superior powers of observation."

"It's about time somebody noticed."

"And perhaps memory. Is there a regular crew that hangs out there on Sundays? And are there Walker's girls who typically show up?"

"Is this about the Mallory Harding thing that everyone knows you're nosing into?"

"Could be."

"Well, I'll try not to answer as many of your questions as I can."

"I've already asked you two."

"Do I get extra credit for this? Oh, shit, I'm not in any of your classes."

"You take math with Mr. Doolan, right? I'll see if I can put in a good word."

"I can do math with my eyes tied behind my back, but whatever."

"So, what have you got?"

"First of all, we don't always go down there. Sometimes we go to the mall or the bowling alley, where we can actually get into trouble. But yes, we go down to the fields more Sundays than not. If it's not winter."

"And 'we' consists of?"

"Oh, Banks, Hennessey, Toomer, Harper, Bazeby, that crowd. Banks and Hennessey always think they're on the verge of getting laid. Do I have to name everyone?"

"Nah, that's good enough. I'm not as interested in the boys."

"Spoken like a true Walker's girl—at least where Banks and Hennessey are concerned."

"What about the Walker's girls? Names?"

"Oh, it's a rotating cast. Lisa McInerney. Meg Marston. Melissa Clark sometimes. Beth Hoffman sometimes. Cathy St. John sometimes. Maggie Duchesne—I think you know her—sometimes. Jody Belanger once in a while. Is that enough names?"

"Could be. But here's something. At least one of Kevin's

kids—maybe Jimmy Harper—actually remembers being at the fields the day Mallory went missing. Does that ring any kind of a bell with you?"

Reese cocked his head, mildly surprised that this much information was getting back to Sam, even though Reese himself was often a key whisperer in the gossip pipeline. On the other hand, Reese liked Sam, and admired his insights, and didn't mind giving him tidbits of info, as long as he could leave something out for possible future use.

Reese sighed, and began to explain. "The reason Jimmy remembered that day," he said, "Is that we had been talking about Mallory. Before the girls got there, we were having a friendly little game of 'Who would you fuck?' Maggie's name came up a lot—you know, the glamorous supermodel looks, the fabulous rack—everything you see in her."

"Reese, come on. Eyes on the ball."

"More like eyes on the boobs. But anyway, Lisa McInerney got votes. So did Melissa Clark. Cathy St. John if you like cute blondes with brains. Not quite a consensus on any of them, but if there was any consensus to be had, it was on Mallory Harding. The whole package. The looks. The allure. The face. The bedroom eyes. And the gorgeous long locks of auburn hair."

"Nobody would have dared taking on Tomas, but every-one wanted to be her next jockey. Once Banks even said—no, he said this more than once—'The second he dumps her for a college girl, I'm all over her like a cheap suit.'"

"I hear Banks is a lot of talk," said Sam.

"Oh? Who told you that?"

"Just a little birdie." Sam smiled. "And then within a couple of days, Mallory is reported missing--"

"And Jimmy Harper feels like shit for including her in the game. That bothered him for a while, you know."

"One more thing, Reese, and I'll make this quick. I know it just kills you to be late for class."

"Like a dagger in my heart. Wait, do I even have a heart?"

"Can you tell me specifically which girls were there that day?"

"Melissa Clark and Maggie Duchesne for sure. Jody Belanger and Lisa McInerney for sure. I think Lisa and Graham Toomer were trading barbs that day, you know, like teen lovebirds do when they're trying to get each other's attention with insults, and next thing you know, they're banging. Yeah, I'm pretty sure they're banging now."

"Anyone else?"

"That's four of them, right? I think there were five. Yeah, Cathy St. John was there too. I'm sure I saw her that day. But I think she left earlier than most of us. I think she thought we were getting too crude."

Reese turned to walk away toward class, then turned back to Sam. "Mr. Field," he whispered. "Don't you want to know who Maggie Duchesne is banging?"

"No, Reese, I don't," he said emphatically.

Reese took two more steps and then turned toward Sam one more time.

"She isn't," he said. "She flirts a lot, but she isn't, you know, doing that."

By now, they were too far apart to have a completely

private conversation. That didn't stop Reese from getting in one more loud whisper.

"She's holding out for you."

Jackie's friend in the registrar's office at UConn told her she could get a private message to Tomas with Jackie's phone number and an invitation to call her about new information she had. Jackie didn't know if the feeler would work, and was surprised when Tomas called her the next day.

"Hi Tomas. Yes, this is Jackie Spellmeyer. I do appreciate your calling me back."

"The message said you have new information. I do know they found her body. Was that it?"

"No, there's one more thing. I know about your drinking with Mallory on Sundays, and the arrangement you had with her if either one of you thought you were too drunk to drive."

"Oh, OK."

"That and the location of the remains suggests you might want to change your story about that day. If you're willing to talk to me before the police put all this together, I can come up to Storrs and get a statement. My gut tells me you lied because you didn't want anyone to know about the drinking. So if you still want to maintain your innocence, you might be able to help me with my investigation of other leads."

After a pause, Tomas replied. "I'm free at three tomorrow, if that works for you. I know a coffee shop near the campus that should be quiet around that time."

Next, Jackie dialed the number Reisa had given her for the office of Comprehensive School Counseling at state ed. Victoria Lavelle seemed surprised and confused that Jackie wanted to talk to her, and further baffled when Jackie recounted to her the story Sam had told her about the bar.

After a pause, she replied sheepishly, "To be honest, I don't really remember what I said."

"Why don't we talk for a few minutes tomorrow at your office," Jackie replied in a calm, soothing tone. "I have to be in Storrs at 3."

Victoria thought for a moment. "Why don't we just meet at my house in Manchester. I can spare a half-hour. I'd rather get out of the office for this."

"Manchester," Jackie repeated aloud. "That would work if you can meet around 1:30."

"Yes, I can do that. Here's my address and home phone."

Victoria opened the door into a modest living room with mostly old furniture and a couple of bowls of candy on wooden end tables. Jackie assessed the thin, angular woman, her face weathered by her lonely and bitter life, and almost immediately concluded that she was an unlikely suspect. But she needed to see how Victoria would respond to Sam's account of her tirade. She listened intently as Jackie walked her through it.

"That girl gave me a hard time," Victoria said finally. "And her mind was made up to think freely and to"—here she choked on the words she had to say—"and to love boys carelessly. There was no talking common sense to her."

"Yes," Jackie said. "I understand she had strong opinions on love and sex. And she spoke her mind. Did that make you angry?"

"And I have to admit," Victoria continued, "she was very

eloquent in her positions, even charismatic. The other girls were just eating out of her hand. Frankly, I didn't think ..."

"Think what?"

"That she was the best role model for the other girls. I guess she can think freely all she wants, but most of them need better guidance at that age. So yes, I was a little ... maybe angry is too strong. Let's just say, put off."

Jackie paused for a moment, almost feeling guilty about the one last question she had to ask. "Enough to make you want to get back at her somehow?"

Victoria's sad and tired eyes flashed a hint of indignation. "God no," she said. "I came to help those girls, not to fight with them. It was a frustrating day, but I put it behind me. I have other clients to serve, and most of them aren't privileged like the Walker's girls."

"OK," Jackie said. "I'm sorry I had to ask." She paused, briefly debating whether to go ahead with what she wanted to say next. But she did go ahead, because she wanted Victoria to know that she while she no longer saw her as a suspect, she did see her as a person, and a complicated one.

"By the way," Jackie added, "Sam filled me in on a little bit of your backstory. I'm sorry about that too."

"Oh, Kieran must have told him. He's such a nice fellow, I can't be mad at him. He takes care of me. Sometimes I wonder who's going to take care of these girls if they get into trouble. Some of them have no idea what's coming."

In Storrs, Jackie and Tomas ordered cups of coffee and took them to a corner table in the mostly quiet shop. "First of all," Tomas began, "I want to be clear that Mallory didn't drink with me, never more than a sip or two. It was just me, blowing off steam from all the pressure I felt at Avon."

"How are things going for you at UConn?" Jackie asked.

Tomas thought for a second. "Actually, it's a lot better for me. It's a lot less pressure, maybe because it's so big. At Avon, I felt like everyone was always watching over me, waiting for me to screw up because maybe I didn't belong there. And here, I don't have my parents breathing down my neck all the time."

"If you don't mind my asking, do you get along?"

"Oh, yeah, no major problems. And I know they love me and want the best for me. But they could be, you know, a little suffocating. I just needed to be someplace where nobody's on me all the time."

"How are you handling the social life? There must be parties, drinking ..."

"Yeah ... Let me say this. The Sunday drinking thing at Avon was a bad habit I fell into. I go to parties here sometimes, but it's not the same thing. It's not a binge thing. So far, I'm handling it well, I think."

"Baseball's a spring sport, right?"

"Yeah, but next spring's captains hold fall workouts. I know all the guys, and the coaches, and I feel welcome here. I know it will come down to producing on the field, but I think ... hope ... I'll be able to handle it."

"All right, let's talk about that day. I'm pretty sure you did not drive Mallory to Walker's. I'm also pretty sure she never made it to Walker's. Based on where her remains were found, I think she might have entered the river somewhere near Avon

Old Farms, maybe at Fisher Meadows. Did you know the river flows northward from there?"

"Yes, I grew up near there, played down by the river as a kid. I also spent a lot of time wandering the park. Knew all the spots."

"Did you and Mallory go there?"

Tomas paused and looked Jackie in the eyes. He had already prepared what he was going to say. He leaned in a little, and began.

"Look, I don't want to lie any more about that day. Not about any of it. Mallory and I did go to Fisher Meadows often, and we were there that day, after driving around a while. We went there to make out. I had already been drinking Jack Daniel's. She liked sex. So did I, big surprise. So we started right in. We did it once and then I sat back up and took another big swig of whiskey. I think that's when it started to go wrong."

"Did you have a fight?"

"I never hit her, never once. But we had an argument. She started talking about how I drank too much. I tried to make excuses. She had accepted my excuses in the past. But this time, she said she was tired of my excuses. I said I thought she understood what I was going through and why I had become dependent on the Sunday drinking. She said she tried to be as understanding as she could, but she was tired of that too. She said maybe I should see someone, get professional help. I got mad and said I didn't need professional help, I'd fix my problems on my own. She told me I was slurring my words."

"I remember her saying that," Tomas continued, "but I

was going downhill. Definitely the most I ever drank. Everything after is kind of a blur. I remember she said she wanted to screw again, and tried to climb on top of me, but I was pretty useless at that point. She started to yell at me again. I think she might have used the word 'useless,' actually. I'm pretty sure she slapped me across the face."

"Had she ever done that before? Did you hit her back?"

"I told you, I never hit her ... After she slapped me, I'm pretty sure I climbed out of the car and staggered around to the passenger side. I think I was holding onto the car for support. She got out of the passenger side, and the door knocked me over. I was struggling to get up. I think she actually pulled me up. I think she was crying and yelling at me—like I said, it was a blur. I can't remember any of what she said at that point. The only thing I'm sure of is that I said I would walk home and that the keys were in the ignition. I think she might have protested and said she'd drive me, but I staggered off. I don't know how, but somehow I regained just enough balance to make it home."

"Do you remember the walk at all?"

"Very little. I'm sure I tried to avoid seeing people, and of course I know all the shortcuts, even when I'm drunk. Some of them go through woods—maybe I used the trees to keep my balance."

"Do you remember seeing anyone?"

"Not really. As I left the park and got closer to the main road, I became vaguely aware of some people over on the soccer fields, off to my right, and my only thought was to not walk near them. And I think there was someone on the path walking in my direction. But I turned and stumbled away from her."

"Her? It was a woman? A girl?"

Tomas squinted his eyes and hunted through his memory for a visual.

"I can't say. Maybe a girl. Actually, I think it was a girl."

"Did you know her?"

Tomas cocked his head and thought for a second. "You know, my very foggy memory tells me I reacted to her as someone I knew. But that's where it ends. I couldn't for the life of me tell you who it was."

"But you got home."

"Yes. I woke up early the next morning, on my bed, in my clothes. No one else was up. I took a shower, got dressed for school, and started walking toward 44. I called a cab at some point, and had him drop me off at the Cobb School. My car was there in the parking lot, so I assumed Mallory made it back OK."

"Nothing else unusual about the car? Nothing you found spilled on the floors or under the seats?"

"I'm sure I didn't look down there. I usually don't. I just wanted to get out of the parking lot before all the parents started dropping off their kids."

"So that's it? Nothing else out of the ordinary?"

"Well--"

"Yes?"

"I'm sure it's nothing."

"You know, Tomas, in my line of work, you learn that no

piece of potential evidence is too small or seemingly minor to ignore."

"It wasn't in the same place."

"Wait--what?"

"Every other time Mallory took the car overnight, she parked to the left of the entrance. More trees there to block the view from the road."

"And this time?"

"It was to the right of the entrance."

"Maybe her usual space was taken."

"It's a day school. No one is there at six o'clock on a Sunday."

"And when you get there in the morning?"

"Teachers are starting to arrive. Like I said, I like to get in and out before the kids get there. But no one has ever said anything to me."

"And the Buick was parked in a different spot than where you usually found it. Did you ever give that much thought?"

"No, not really. I was going to ask Mallory about it. Obviously, I never got the chance."

Chapter 19

August 1983

The summer is waning, so of course I'm finally feeling close to someone I'll have to say goodbye to soon. It's probably just as well. But it's nice to feel my heart for a change.

Adam made love to me tonight on the beach. It was getting cool, so there weren't many people out, and we laid out a big beach towel in between some rocks. No one could see us from the road, and we could hear the surf rolling gently onto the shore just beyond us. He said let's go slowly and follow the rhythm of the waves, and we did, and we kept our breath as quiet as possible so we could listen, and the sensations were just amazing. Keeping our sweatshirts on somehow made it even more intimate. He will leave me with that lovely memory.

"Only in the agony of parting do we look into the depths of love," wrote George Eliot, and I fear she may be right. The love I feel right now may be fleeting, but it is stronger for having to let it go.

These boys are passing pleasures anyway compared with the depths of love I have looked into, lost now forever, whose agony will not go away and cannot be measured.

December 1983

Sam had gone back and forth on whether to include Warren in the pizza outing. He would have preferred not to, so he could ask the girls questions without the distraction of having one of their boyfriends there. Maybe he was feeling guilty that his relationship with Maggie had (temporarily, at least) had overstepped its proper boundary, but in the end, he decided to invite Warren to dilute any suspicion over what an adult male teacher was doing socializing alone with three teenage girls.

Sam drove Warren to a spacious restaurant on Route 44 that specialized in pizza, subs and conventional Southern Italian entrees. Sam had made a reservation, and they were led to a round table with five seats. When the girls arrived separately, Warren stood up to help them with their coats. Maggie got to the table first and chose a seat that left one between her and Sam, who quickly said, "I hope this isn't going to be uncomfortable for you."

"How will it not be uncomfortable for me?" she replied, flashing him a smile.

"Well, anyhow, it's nice to see you," he said.

"Nice to see you too."

The others returned; Suzanne took the seat between Maggie and Sam, leaving Warren and Annie to sit next to each other.

A server appeared who looked to be in her mid 30s or so. She announced that her name was Becky and that she'd be taking care of the table, and took drink orders—mostly water and soda, and an iced tea for Sam. After Becky left to fetch the drinks, the party discussed the menu and quickly decided to share two large pizzas with various toppings.

"How was everyone's Thanksgiving?" Sam asked in a not-very-successful attempt to start a conversation. Mostly they nodded and gave short answers. He turned to Suzanne and said, "You know, I spent a whole week in Northampton. Were you around?"

"A couple of nights in South Hadley with my family, but then a couple of girlfriends and I went to Boston for the weekend."

"Did you see Katie?" asked Annie.

"Just once," he said, staring back at her in a way that he hoped would project that he wanted to stay off this subject. "Pizza and drinks. It was nice to catch up."

"Who's Katie?" asked Maggie.

"Oh," he replied, struggling to sound nonchalant. "Just an old girlfriend from high school. We're good friends now."

"Hey," he continued. "How was New York?"

"It was wonderful," Maggie replied. "It always is. New York at Christmastime is magical."

After a pause, she added, "Of course, the end of the week was a major bummer."

"Oh, yeah, of course," he replied, and then paused before continuing. "And I just want to emphasize how sorry I am about what happened, and that you all had to go through this awful time."

All of them murmured "Thank you."

Maggie spoke up again. "I suppose," she said. "It's better now that we know. All of those weeks and months of not knowing, and fearing the worst, and trying to keep our feelings inside."

"Did anyone try to get help? Counseling?"

Suzanne raised her hand.

"I saw the counselor here at the school once," she said. "It helped a little. Summer break helped more. I was lucky—I already had a trip planned. One of those outdoor excursions where you basically inhabit a totally different world for three weeks."

"Oh, wow, that sounds pretty cool," Sam said. "Where did you go?"

"Northern Minnesota at the Canadian border. An area they call the Boundary Waters. It's beautiful. So many lakes. Lots of canoeing, some community service. I'd never trade the experience for anything."

"Great. Anyone else have an interesting summer?"

"Not me," said Annie. "I mean not like that. I worked as a part-time lifeguard on the New Hampshire shore, and also at a restaurant in Portsmouth. Summer is the busy season. Now Maggie, at least she got to work someplace interesting.'

"It was a summer internship," Maggie said. "At Christie's. The auction house. Yeah, I guess you could say that was interesting."

"Warren, you can speak once in a while if you want," said Sam, smiling.

Warren laughed and said he painted houses in Albany with his older brother.

"Really," said Sam. "I painted houses in Northampton with a friend for about a month and a half. I left the ad agency in June, and didn't have to be here until late August."

"I know a couple of teachers here who paint houses in the summer," Warren said. "They have the time off, so why not?"

Becky arrived and took the orders for pizza and salads.

Sam cleared his throat. "Well, you all know by now that I'm helping Inspector Spellmeyer, the P.I. Mallory's parents hired, with her case. And based on further evidence we have collected, we decided to ask her closest friends a few more questions to see if we can develop any new leads. I'm not trying to upset anyone, but I think we'd all like to get this resolved."

"Is Tomas still considered a suspect?" asked Annie.

"I'm sure the police will take another hard look at him, now that they found her. I don't blame them, but Mrs. Spellmeyer has already talked to him again, and for reasons I can't get into right now, neither of us thinks he's guilty."

"So," Sam continued, "I'll start with the obvious, including questions you probably answered before. Did she have any enemies that you know of? Jealous would-be boyfriends she turned away?"

"Enemies?" Annie looked around at the other girls, who shrugged their shoulders. "She really didn't have enemies to speak of. More like admirers. She wasn't the type of girl to be critical, or to rub people the wrong way."

"Lots of Avon boys were attracted to her," said Maggie. "But it was almost this thing where they deferred to Tomas, who also was well-liked and well-respected at the school. And he was graduating, while Mallory would have been here one more year. I know one boy at least who said he was going to go after her once Tomas went off to college."

"Banks?" asked Sam.

"Yes!" Maggie exclaimed. "How did you--"

"Gossip spreads quickly at Avon, if you hadn't noticed. And now that I have a couple of good sources ... Well, never mind that. I want to go back to something else you said. That Tomas was well-liked and respected at the school. I don't doubt it, but did he know that? From some things you guys said, and also Mrs. Spellmeyer, I got the feeling he felt a lot of pressure here."

Annie and Maggie shot each other knowing looks.

"The parents," Annie said.

"Tomas' parents?" Sam asked.

"They meant well," said Maggie. "But compared to a lot of Avon families, they're more working-class. They worried that he wouldn't fit in. He cooks in an Italian restaurant— holy shit."

"What?" Sam asked.

"Oh my god," Maggie said. "This couldn't be the one, could it?"

The swinging doors leading into the kitchen were at the other end of the dining room, and did not really offer a glimpse inside.

"I really have no idea," said Sam.

Just then Becky appeared with a large tray, and the conversation stopped completely until all the food was on the table and she finished pouring refills.

"Anyway," Maggie continued, "They projected their own doubts onto him. He's tough, but I don't think he could help but soak some of that in. He internalizes it."

"Unlike his little brother," said Suzanne, "who comes out swinging."

"Suzanne," Sam said, turning to her, "maybe you can help with a couple of specific questions about Mallory, since you lived with her."

"Well, we all lived together in so many ways, but yes, I was her roommate."

"First of all, and this may sound like an odd question, but I've been learning from Mrs. Spellmeyer to look around every imaginable corner. Is there any possibility that Mallory was getting interested in a new boy, or was thinking of breaking up with Tomas?"

The girls all looked around at each other like Sam had asked them if the earth is flat.

"She adored him," said Maggie. "I can tell you that right up until that day, she couldn't wait to spend the day with him on Sundays."

"And she had no qualms about bragging that he was the best ever," said Annie.

"Annie!" scolded Maggie.

"Oh come on," said Annie. "Don't be such a prude. I think Mr. Field and Mrs. Spellmeyer would want to know, for their investigation, that Mallory loved sex and was very impressed with Tomas' ... um ... abilities."

"I will add only that Mallory was a progressive thinker," said Suzanne, "and it bothered her anytime a girl or a woman was shamed for liking sex or for wearing clothing that showed anything off."

"Not that you can do that here anyway," added Maggie. "Mr. Field, did you know the rules here don't even allow the girls to sunbathe?"

The girls giggled. Warren just smiled.

"Now, changing the subject, Suzanne, one more thing," said Sam. "Did Mallory keep a journal?"

"A journal?" she asked, puzzled.

"You know, like a diary. Like a little book she wrote in before going to bed."

Suzanne cocked her head and thought it over, before looking around at the other girls for help. They just shrugged their shoulders.

Suzanne finally spoke. "No, I don't remember anything like that. At bedtime, on school nights at least, we'd talk and joke and then turn out our lights at the same time."

"Hmm," said Sam. "Was she a good writer?"

Again, the girls all looked around at each other and shrugged their shoulders.

"She was smart," said Annie finally. "And she had decent grades. So I'm sure she did well in English comp and English lit. Why do you ask?"

"Oh, I have a reason," said Sam. "But it's probably nothing. Are all the girls in your group smart? Smart students tend to hang out together."

"Yes, I would agree with that," said Maggie. "But then, you have to be pretty smart to get into Walker's in the first place."

"What English classes are you all taking this year?" Sam asked.

"Honors English," answered Maggie and Annie in unison.

"Both of you? Same class?"

"Yeah," said Annie. Suzanne raised her hand.

"You too? What about the other girls? Are you all in the same English class?"

"Melissa Clark and Beth Hoffman are in the other Honors English class. There are two sections."

Sam did a mental count in his head—someone was missing.

"What about Cathy St. John?" he asked.

The girls looked at each other and smiled.

"No, not Honors English," said Maggie.

"Oh," said Sam, sounding vaguely disappointed.

"Advanced Placement English," Maggie continued. "She's a little too smart for the rest of us."

Sam perked up again. "Isn't she the one from Long Island?" he asked. "Northport, I think she said. Near Stony Brook."

"Yeah, her mother's an English professor there," said Annie.

"Reading books since she was a little girl," Maggie added. "Her parents basically let her read anything. And of course, there are books all over the house."

"Of course, of course," repeated Sam, momentarily lost in thought.

Snapping back to attention, he asked, "And what does her father do?"

"He's a senior writer for *Newsday*," said Annie.

"Smart, literate family," said Sam.

"Busy family," remarked Annie. "Cathy once joked that they probably gave her so many books to read so that they wouldn't have to spend time with her. Then again, maybe she wasn't joking."

"And I suppose Cathy can probably write," said Sam, trying to sound nonchalant.

Again, the girls looked at each other and smiled, until Maggie spoke.

"Well, she won the junior essay contest last year."

The check came, and Sam tried to wind down the discussion with a return to more trivial matters.

In the restaurant's kitchen, Mario Arpante went to work on another order, oblivious to the meeting that had just taken place.

Back in his apartment, Sam dialed Jackie's number.

"Interesting conversation at the pizza place tonight," he said. "With a couple of new details that might help us pull together the various strands of the case. But I'm still a little hazy on things like what actually happened, motive, and so on. I have a hunch or two, and a theory that maybe, just maybe, it was an unpremeditated crime of passion. Wow. Crazy."

"Not too crazy," Jackie replied. "But still hazy, like you said. I have a hunch or two myself—a few things Reisa and the girls said early on stand out in my mind now. I took good notes. I need to speak to Reisa again. And to talk to a few more of those girls."

"If I'm anywhere close," said Sam, "we're going to have to

figure out a way to put a plausible timeline together. Can we meet tomorrow?"

"Sure, what time is good for you? And by the way, I saw the pathology report. Blunt force trauma to the back of the skull. I don't know if I'm off-base to say this, but it might be consistent with the big round dent in Tomas' passenger side door."

No sooner had Sam hung up the phone than it rang again. He thought it would be Jackie with something she forgot to tell him.

It was Maggie.

"I have to see you. Alone. There's something I need to tell you, and I don't want the other girls around. I can't believe I'm saying this, but I haven't even told Annie. And don't worry, it's not a trap."

"OK, when?"

"I'm busy all day Saturday, but I could sneak away Sunday, maybe late afternoon, and meet you over at the Cobb School parking lot."

"Perfect," said Sam, as he suddenly realized he had other business to take care of there too, business he could conduct only on Sunday.

Chapter 20

August 1983

We were never lovers, only friends. But in my own shy way, I think I asked too much. I wanted to be around you all the time, a satellite orbiting the most brilliant star in the sky. A timid orchid in your beautiful garden, leaning in to be closer to the queen of all roses. A needy friend waiting patiently but desperately for you to need me back.

I should have listened to Toni Morrison. "Did you ever see the way the clouds love a mountain? They circle all around it; sometimes you can't even see the mountain for the clouds. But you know what? You go up top and what do you see? His head. The clouds never cover the head. His head pokes through, because the clouds let him; they don't wrap him up."

I wanted to love you like the clouds love a mountain. Wrapping myself around your aura, but letting you breathe. What I wouldn't give to let you breathe again.

December 1983

On Friday, Sam's last class ended at 3 o'clock, after which

he drove over to the Spellmeyer home. Jackie had just let him in when the phone rang. It was Reisa Maitlin returning her call.

"Hi Jackie, how are you? Reisa began.

"Doing well, how about you?" Jackie said.

"Oh, about the same as ever," she replied. "Can't complain."

"That's good. Hey listen, I have another favor to ask. Sorry to bother you again, but our investigation has turned up a few interesting new leads. I'd like you to arrange a meeting for me —maybe half an hour—with a couple of the other girls."

Reisa sighed.

"Well, we are trying to get back to some semblance of normal here. But I guess I can do that. Do you know the ones you want this time?"

"I was thinking the two girls who dropped equestrian this year. Suzanne Fiorini and Cathy St. John."

"OK, what should I tell them? Same as I told Annie and Maggie when you met with them?"

"The other girls know I met with Annie and Maggie, right?"

"Do they? I'm not sure who knows what at this point."

"Just tell them I'm interviewing the girls two at a time to make sure we cover all bases in the investigation."

"OK, I'll do that," Reisa said, followed by a pause.

"You don't think any of them is a suspect, do you?"

Jackie lowered her tone, as she often did an almost subconscious attempt to soothe people she was giving bad news to.

"Reisa, I have to be honest with you. New information has

surfaced that forces us to widen the net. There are possible scenarios that might involve someone in the Walker's family. But I'm not ready to show my hand yet."

Reisa, worried, didn't speak at first. Finally, she said, "I understand."

"Please let me know when you can make them available. The sooner the better. I'm sorry this is weighing on the school the way it is. But as I'm sure you understand, I'm doing this for closure for Mallory's family."

After Jackie hung up the receiver, Sam said, "OK let's talk about a timeline. And make sure we shared all of the info we have. What do we know about that day?"

"Well," Jackie began, "Tomas picked up Mallory at Walker's shortly after Sunday brunch. They went for a drive —Brad Sullivan mentioned Westfarms Mall, but I'm not even concerned about that now. The important thing is that sometime in midafternoon or so, they parked the car somewhere in Fisher Meadows."

"And Tomas was drinking," said Sam. "He admits that now, right?"

"Yes," Jackie confirmed. "They had sex. Then he started drinking some more, and he told me that shortly thereafter, it all fell apart."

"She wanted to have sex again," Jackie continued. But he was wrecked by the time she tried to do it again, and it was no use. The way Tomas described it, they had argued about his drinking before, but this time it got uglier. She said she was tired of his excuses, called him 'useless,' and smacked him across the face. That's when he got out of the car."

"And he told you he stumbled around to the passenger side," said Sam, standing up and staggering around the end of the dining room table, both hands clutching it, to imitate the action.

"But that's when Mallory opened the door and knocked him over," Jackie said, while Sam flung himself backward onto an easy chair.

"And he somehow got up and staggered off," she added. "The only other detail he recalled is that someone was coming toward him down the path. He said he thought he knew the person but couldn't quite make her out."

"Her," Sam repeated. "He thought it was a girl."

"So we don't know what happened next," Sam continued. "And if it was a girl, we don't know which one."

"True," Jackie said, "but you indicated you might have a hunch."

"Well, I do know that Reese said Cathy St. John was hanging out at the soccer fields that day, and left the group early. He was a little hazy on when she left and which way she went, but that's something."

"The other thing I found out last night is that Cathy is the star writer of the group," Sam added. "She won the junior essay contest at Walker's."

"Some of those journal entries I read were very artfully crafted, in my humble opinion," said Jackie. "Written by someone who thinks about what they're writing and has some literary technique."

"None of the girls, not even her roommate, could remember Mallory ever keeping a journal," Sam said. "So I got them talking about their English classes, and that's when I found out most of them are taking Honors English—except Cathy, who's in Advanced Placement."

"And we also know," Sam continued, "that she grew up in a home full of books, with an English professor mother and a journalist father—who, I'm told, didn't have a lot of time for her. Books may have been her solace. She probably read *Wuthering Heights* when she was nine."

"So we might be able to connect Cathy with the writing in the journal I found in the car," Jackie said, "especially if we can locate a current journal she's been keeping ... Oh, damn."

"What?" said Sam.

"The items in the car. When I first gathered them up, I wasn't thinking about the possibility of them belonging to a different girl, someone who was nervous and in a hurry and might have spilled things out of her bag. There was a hairbrush--"

Sam's eyes widened. "Which might have blonde hair in it!"

"Wow," said Jackie. "The journal, and a couple of strands of blonde hair in that brush, and we have a case."

"OK, I think we've connected about 75 percent of the dots," Sam said. "I think it's possible that Cathy had an unhealthy obsession with Mallory. How to prove that ..."

"There are a couple of interesting things in my notes," Jackie said. "I may not have told you this, because at the time, I wasn't sure if it would be important. Around Thanksgiving of junior year, Mallory sank into depression, which was unlike her. Her parents were fighting and considering a divorce. The person who gave most of her time and helped her through it was Cathy St. John."

"Now on the face of it," Jackie continued, "that might seem like positive, empathetic behavior. Can there be a dark side to that? I have read some things on this over the years. Sometimes desperate, needy people obsessed with another person look for opportunities to be that person's guardian angel. They show them an overabundance of love and care—because they are longing to have the same amount of love and care given back. And this can be especially true if they feel unloved at home."

For the second time during the fall semester, Reisa led Jackie into an unoccupied faculty apartment where two girls in plaid skirts and white blouses were waiting. Jackie introduced herself, took a notepad and pen out of her bag, and quickly sized them up. Both of the girls looked athletic; Suzanne was taller, with brown hair, dark brown eyes, and olive-toned Mediterranean skin. Cathy had straw-blonde hair, greenish blue eyes and a paler skin tone. Jackie noted that Cathy, while only about 5-foot-4, had nicely toned calf muscles, and appeared to have strong shoulders that filled out her blouse.

"I want to begin by saying how sorry I am for all of you girls, having to endure this awful time and the loss of your friend. I'm still trying to piece together what happened that day, and I'm trying to meet with all of the girls in Mallory's circle to gather potential leads. I'm not sure if you know, but I already met with Annie Green and Maggie Duchesne."

Both girls nodded in apparent confirmation that they knew, though neither spoke up.

"OK, and you may also know that an Avon teacher, Mr. Field, has been assisting me in this case."

Both girls nodded again.

"In fact, he told me that you, Suzanne, took an interesting trip last summer that helped you get your mind off Mallory for a while. Canoeing up in northern Minnesota?"

"Yeah," Suzanne said. "It was one of those organized youth excursions. And it was amazing. Beautiful area—they call it the Boundary Waters."

"Oh, right," Jackie said, "All those lakes near the U.S.-Canadian border. I was up that way for a few days once, quite some time ago. Did you have to do any training prior to the trip?"

"Not really. They teach you canoeing and portaging skills as you go, especially in the first several days. I was already WSI-certified, but that wasn't required of the students."

"WSI?" Jackie asked.

"Water Safety Instruction," said Cathy.

Jackie turned to Cathy. "Are you WSI-certified too?"

"Yeah, and Lifeguard-certified."

"Were you a lifeguard over the summer?

"I worked at a club in the Hamptons. I did a little bit of everything—lifeguard, swim instructor, tennis instructor. It was fun. I like the kids most of the time."

"So you must be a good swimmer and tennis player!"

"I guess so. My parents signed me up for lessons at a club near our house when I was pretty young. My mother wanted me to get outside and do athletic things so I wouldn't just stay in and read all the time. I got good pretty quickly, and soon I was teaching other kids. As soon as my mother could drop me off at the club for the day, she went back to her job full-time."

"English professor, I hear."

"Yeah, Stony Brook."

"You like to read?"

"Ever since I was a little girl. I always had a book with me."

"Well, back to Mallory. Did either of you know anyone who considered her an enemy, or had any reason to want to hurt her?"

The girls looked at each other, then shook their heads.

Jackie continued with her routine questions. Cathy, who had seemed relaxed and open when talking about her life on Long Island, seemed more withdrawn when the conversation turned to Mallory. Still, she maintained a certain poise throughout.

Jackie had learned one new thing she thought might be useful. And she had one more question to ask.

"Why did you both quit equestrian this year?"

Again, the girls looked at each other. Suzanne spoke first."

"You know I was Mallory's roommate, right? So that already left a big hole in my life. For my own sanity, I avoided any reminders of her that I could. Equestrian was a huge reminder, and I just couldn't do it."

"Cathy?"

For the first time in the interview, Cathy's eyes widened and her face seemed to turn ashen. She said nothing, though her lips parted as if she were trying to form words. Then the tears appeared: big, round tears that rolled down her cheeks, one at a time at first, until they became a flood, and she began to sob softly, lowering her face into her hands.

"That's enough for today," said Jackie, standing up. "Thank you for your help. Again, I am so, so sorry."

Sam and Maggie had agreed to meet in the Cobb School lot at 7. Sam arrived in his Capri at 6:30 and waited for signs of the maintenance man. After about 10 minutes, the same man he had seen on his previous visit emerged from one of the buildings.

"Sir," Sam called out as he walked toward him. "Sorry to bother you--"

"What's up?" the man asked, nicely enough, but with an undercurrent of impatience.

"My name is Sam Field. I'm working with a local private investigator on a missing persons case. You may have seen something here in this parking lot that would be of help to us."

"I'm not sure what you mean," the man answered. "I don't recall seeing anything unusual here."

"Are you always here on Sundays?"

"Yeah, I work a short shift on Sundays, from about 3 till 8. Not that much to do, but I'm the only one here."

"Last spring too?"

"Been here almost eight years now. What's up?"

"At around this time of day, maybe a little earlier, have you ever seen an old Buick Riviera pull in and park here?

He thought for a second. "Yeah, now that you mention it,

I think I do remember that car. It was an old Riviera, probably early '70s. My brother had one like that."

"Did this happen often? And did you see who got out of the car?"

"Several times, I think. Same car, but a different girl each time."

"Different girls?"

"Yeah, definitely not the same one each time. They park, then head across the street. Must go to that boarding school. I always wondered why they parked here."

"Maybe it was two different girls."

"At least. I remember a blonde and a brunette. Maybe her hair was a little reddish. And now that you mention it, I don't think I've seen them in a while."

"So definitely a blonde and a brunette, at least," Sam clarified.

"Yeah, that seems right."

"Thank you," said Sam.

"Sure," he said, turning back toward the building.

"Oh, one more thing," Sam said. "I'll be here a little while longer. I have to meet someone, then I'll be on my way. I don't want you to think I'm up to anything."

The man shrugged his shoulders and kept walking.

Back in his car, Sam looked down at his watch just as it turned 7 o'clock. And sure enough, right then there was a tap on his window. "Get in," Sam said.

Maggie closed the door and looked at Sam, her eyes wide.

"You're trembling," he said.

"I'm sorry I didn't tell you this sooner," she said. "I've

known since May. No one else knows, not even Annie. I just didn't think ..."

"Go on."

"I just didn't think it would turn out to be important. And I didn't think it could possibly be her."

"Her?"

"Cathy. And then, the other night, your line of questioning. When you started asking if people kept journals or were good writers. And I noticed how you perked up when you found out what Cathy's family was like and that she won the junior essay contest. I'm no detective, but I got the distinct feeling you and Mrs. Spellmeyer must have found a journal in Tomas' car."

Sam looked at Maggie and smiled. "You may not be a detective, but you're pretty good."

"The writing in it is very good," Sam continued. "Thoughtful, well-crafted, emotional, with literary undertones. She quotes authors."

"That's Cathy," Maggie said. "There's no one else it could be."

"But what is it that you've known since May?" Sam asked.

Maggie paused. "Mallory came to me for advice. I think she trusted me the most, and she knew I'd keep my word not to tell anyone else. That's why she didn't tell Annie, and made me promise not to tell her."

"Advice about what?"

"What to do about Cathy. She was starting to suffocate her. Cathy accepted that Mallory had a boyfriend, but when she wasn't with Tomas, Cathy wanted to be with her all the time. She had become so needy. Ever since she helped Mallory through her depression—she was great then, by the way—she kind of expected Mallory to return the favor and treat her like the most special girl in the group. And Mallory wasn't like that. So she'd push Cathy away gently, and that only made it worse."

"Then one day Cathy came to her room, and set down her bag on a chair. She fumbled in it for something—makeup, maybe—and excused herself to use the bathroom. That's when Mallory noticed what looked like Cathy's journal, and decided to take a peek. When she saw the things Cathy was writing, she said to herself, *This has to stop.*"

"That's right," Maggie continued," I knew about the journal when you brought it up at the restaurant. But I couldn't say anything."

"So what was your advice?"

"I told Mallory to tell Cathy she needed a complete break. Kind of like breaking up with a boyfriend. For the time being anyway. I suggested that she mention how grateful she was for her support, but that the friendship needed a timeout if they wanted to stay friends down the road. And she couldn't be gentle about it."

"And do you know what happened?"

"I mean, I didn't see her do it. But I'm pretty sure she did. Cathy was very gloomy after that. And a couple of weeks later, Mallory went missing."

"Holy shit," Sam said. "That's it. The last piece. Thank you."

Sam looked at Maggie, whose eyes were still wide. She looked frightened.

"Oh Jesus," he said. "I wasn't even thinking about your feelings. This must be awful for you. Cathy is your friend too."

"I know," Maggie said, brushing away a tear. "It feels terrible. But I had to say something to you. There was no other choice."

"I know," Sam said. "And I'm so sorry. But you made the right choice."

After a pause, Maggie whispered, "Mr. Field?"

"Yes?"

"I want you to know I have never forgotten our kiss."

Sam sighed, taken by surprise, torn again about his feelings, and wondering how to reply.

"Yes, I haven't forgotten it either. But I have to be professional about things, you know?"

"Yes, I know."

In the minute of silence that followed, Maggie placed her hand upon Sam's.

"Mr. Field?" she said, as he allowed her to caress his hand.

"Yes?"

"I have a favor to ask."

"Ask away."

"I'm having a hard time pretending I don't have feelings for you, but I have to learn to put them aside. In order to do that, I'd like one more little memory. Can I ask you to be unprofessional for just one more minute? Nobody will know."

Torn between competing impulses, Sam looked at her and

said nothing, but allowed her to slowly lean over to him until he could feel her breath upon his face. Their lips met and they kissed feverishly for a long minute—or maybe two or three minutes, Sam thought as he finally, gently, pulled his mouth back from hers.

"I don't know what to do with you," he said.

Maggie got out of the car, but just as Sam was about to drive away, he heard another tap on his window.

He rolled it down and saw that she was smiling impishly at him.

"Guess what?" she asked.

"I don't know, what?"

"In six months, I'll be graduated, and I'll be 18! Now let's see, Annie always says I'm 17 going on 25, so I guess that means I'll be 26! I'll be older than you!"

Maggie laughed and skipped away across the road and over to Ethel Walker School.

Chapter 21

October 1983

I am here again and you are not.

I pass the time and do the work and try to forget.

I close my eyes at night and try not to hear your voice in my head.

It's no use.

Virginia Woolf wrote, "I see you everywhere, in the stars, in the river; to me you're everything that exists; the reality of everything."

Of all the quotes I've written down, I think this one hits the closest to home.

I see you everywhere, in the stars, in the river.

In the stars, in the river.

Lord have mercy on my soul.

December 1983

"Dear mother of God," said Reisa Maitlin under her breath as a Chevy Impala with a Hartford County Sheriff's logo pulled up in front of Beaver Brook. Jackie Spellmeyer and Sam Field got out, along with Sheriff Dn Masterson.

Reisa knew they were coming; Jackie had warned her. Reisa walked up to them, and Jackie immediately introduced Masterson, who then said, "We have a warrant to search the room of Cathy St. John for certain items that may be relevant to the Mallory Harding case."

"Smith Dorm, over here," Reisa said, and led the way. "Cathy rooms with a postgrad student named Sarah Voelker. Hard to say whether either of them will be there."

Students and faculty who were outside at that moment stared at the procession as they walked to Smith.

Masterson knocked on the door of Cathy's second-floor room. There was no answer; he knocked one more time, and they waited a couple of minutes.

"I brought a master with me," said Reisa, unlocking the door and then turning to leave. "I hope this goes as well as can be expected."

It looked like a girls' dorm room, with colorful comforters and pillows on the beds, and posters on the walls that ranged from a map of the world to Al Pacino to literary faces next to their memorable quotes. There was a lacrosse stick and a tennis racquet in one corner. The bookshelves were over-flowing; the desks were covered with notebooks, assignment reminders, and writing pads. Jackie and Sam were both trying to figure out which desk was Cathy's when the door opened, and Cathy stood there, startled.

"Please, Cathy, do come in," said Jackie. "We have a warrant to search your room."

Masterson held up the warrant.

"But ... why?" asked Cathy, her face turning ashen.

"We think you may have items or information that will help us solve the Mallory Harding case," Jackie continued.

"Like your journal," said Sam.

Cathy sat down on her bed, her heart pounding so loudly she thought it might burst through her chest. She began to take deep breaths. "Are you OK?" asked Sam.

"Just let me catch my breath," she half-whispered, half-sobbed, as she considered her options. Maybe it was time. One thing she knew for sure, she was tired of living like a ghost.

"We think we know what happened," said Jackie. "I also suspect you may be tired of hiding it. It took us a while, but the clues are adding up. Mr. Field and I will lay it out for you, if that's OK."

Cathy looked up, her eyes big and moist. "OK, she said, go ahead. Just ... go ahead."

"That Sunday afternoon, you were down on the Avon soccer fields," began Sam. "Hanging out with a bunch of Walker's girls and Avon boys—I won't go through all the names. I have talked to a few of them. But you didn't stay with them—you left early."

Jackie took over. "I have a hunch that you saw Tomas and Mallory drive by. In fact, you may have been the one who called in to the *Hartford Courant* tip line. You knew they were over in Fisher Meadows, parking. Maybe you sensed that something was wrong, maybe you heard something, or maybe you were just in a bad state of mind and decided to throw caution to the wind."

Cathy looked up at Jackie and mouthed, "How did you know?"

Sam cleared his throat, and began speaking. "We know you wanted to be closer to Mallory. You were drawn to her, as apparently a lot of people were. But you took it too far, and you knew it. That didn't stop you from being hurt—maybe even enraged—when she told you to stay away from her. Mallory confided to one—just one—friend in your group. The friend didn't want to tell me at first. She's your friend too. She cares about you, and she didn't want to believe it had anything to do with what happened. But then I said something that made her realize she needed to tell me."

"When you got closer to where the car was," Jackie picked up, "maybe you heard them fighting. Mallory was angry at Tomas because he was drinking too much. Tomas gave me an account of their argument as best he could remember. He says he left the keys in the ignition and stumbled home. Their plan was the one they always used when he was too drunk to drive--that Mallory would drive herself back to school. Tomas vaguely remembered seeing a girl coming down the path toward him, but he staggered off in the other direction. Maybe that girl was you."

Sam: "When you got to the car, Mallory was standing outside of it on the passenger side. She might have been crying. Maybe you saw an opening—we know that you were very generous with your time and care when Mallory went through a depression. So maybe you thought you could show some compassion and win her back as a friend. But I don't think that's what happened. I don't think she was in any mood to see you. Maybe she insulted you. And maybe what she said enraged you. Something went wrong. You must have had some kind of physical fight."

Jackie: "You're obviously not big or tall, but you have a swimmer's strong arms and shoulders. My hunch is that, in your anger, you pushed her hard—maybe even harder than you meant to—and she fell backward and hit the back of her head on the passenger side door. There's a big round dent there now, and the cause of death was blunt force trauma to the back of her skull."

"Then, you panicked," Jackie continued. "You had to take your shoulder bag off and put it in the car, but with Mallory partially blocking the door, you must have tossed or wedged it in at an awkward angle and it flopped over, spilling the contents."

Sam: "Now you had to act fast. You took her pulse first to make sure. We believe you knew how to do that from your Red Cross training. When you knew she was dead, you dragged her to the river, which was not far. We're not sure what you did then, but somehow her body got stuck in the rocks and didn't move for a long time. And somehow, nobody saw you."

Jackie: "You must have been shaking something awful. You got in the car and tried to scoop up the things that fell out of your bag. But some of them fell under the seat or down the crack behind it. And you were too flustered to take inventory."

Sam: "And off you drove to Walker's. You must have known about their little driver switch-up. And that Mallory parked the car at the Montessori school. Annie knew because she's a busybody and she confronted Mallory about it directly. But you were in the spring play with Annie. And you were always keeping an eye on Mallory. Rather than confront her, we suspect you waited for her to pass the theater, and then snuck over to find that Tomas' Buick was parked there. The maintenance guy I spoke with didn't remember everything, but he remembered that at least two different girls sometimes parked the car there—a brunette and a blonde."

Jackie: "And I'm afraid you missed one detail. You didn't park where Mallory always parked."

"Oh," she added, "And speaking of blonde, the hair brush we found under the seat has blonde hair in it, But that wasn't the biggest clue we found in Tomas' car."

At that, Sheriff Masterson pulled the journal out of his pocket. Cathy gasped.

"So," Jackie continued, "If there's a more recent journal in your desk drawer, and the writing style is similar to this one, I'd say the clues all fall into place."

Cathy, still seated on the bed, looked at the three of them in turn, then looked down, then lifted her head and looked straight ahead. The others could sense a new resolve in her—maybe she just wanted to get it over with.

"I'm so tired," Cathy said finally. "I don't want to live like this any more."

Sheriff Masterson quickly said, "You can have a lawyer present when you tell your story. You don't have to say anything now if you don't want to."

"It's OK," Cathy said. "You've put it all together. I'm not

sure how you did it, but I'm actually kind of glad you did. I've been living like a ghost for the last six months. It wears on you—it makes you wonder where your soul went. If it's even still in there."

Cathy looked around at everyone, then focused on Jackie Spellmeyer. "I just want you all to know that I never meant to do this. I loved her so much. Yes, it was obsessive. I couldn't get her out of my head. And then when she told me … "

Cathy began to sob. She stood up and stumbled into the bathroom to get a towel. When she came back, she was wiping her face with it. When she was done, she threw it on her bed, then reached into her desk drawer, pulled out her current journal, and handed it to Jackie.

"When she told me to stay away," Cathy continued, now more composed, "I can't even describe how hurt I was. It was horrible. I remember thinking I wanted to die. Come to think of it, I wish it had been me, not her, who died."

"I heard, and then saw, maybe the last five minutes of their fight. She was so mad at him for being so drunk. I think she was hitting him. He was staggering around like a prize-fighter who had taken one too many punches. Then he just stumbled away."

"And you're right, I thought, now's my chance. Maybe I can be her savior again. When I was helping her with her de-pression over her parents, she was so kind and tender with me. It seemed to mean so much to her. Lots of hugs. And by the way--" here Cathy stopped to stifle a couple of sobs--"we were never sexual lovers or anything. But my heart filled up with the warmth and emotion we were giving to each other. I have never in my life been treated that nicely or felt so special."

"When I came running up to her at the car, she was crying. I reached out my arms, but she pushed them away and yelled "What the fuck are you doing here? Are you still stalking me?"

"I said, 'I was just trying to help you.'"

"Well, you can help me by getting out of my sight, you pathetic creep."

"That was too much. That's when I charged her. I didn't mean to make her fall like that. I'm so, so sorry. So very, very, eternally sorry."

Jackie, who had been alternately watching and listening to Cathy's story and then looking down at her journal, said, "Cathy, these entries are so well-written. Just like the ones we found in the car. We know you're one of the best writers at the school. There is no doubt the two journals were written by the same person. And that person is you."

"Well, Miss St. John," said Sheriff Masterson, "We are going to have to take you in for processing. Involuntary manslaughter. It's not murder, but it's still a crime. You won't have to enter a plea yet. I don't know what will happen, between your age and the possibility of a plea bargain. When we get to the sheriff's office, you can call your parents on Long Island. They can post bail, and you should get an attorney as soon as possible."

"Can I have a few minutes to wash up and change?" asked Cathy.

"Of course," said Masterson. "We'll be right outside."

As the others left, Jackie stayed in the room and closed the door behind her.

"Cathy," she began. "I know this has been a very emotional ordeal for you. And between you and me, I believe you never meant it to end the way it did. I can't say too much more right now. The Hardings are my clients. How they take this news is anybody's guess. And while I don't know exactly what the system will have in store for you, I do know from many years of doing this that some people convicted of far worse crimes have led productive lives on the other side of their sentences. You have a gift that may be very useful to you in your life after this. I hope you will allow that to be a light shining through to give you some hope during the darkest part of your journey. Godspeed."

Cathy looked up, her wide, tear-soaked eyes looking directly at Jackie's. "Mrs. Spellmeyer," she said, measuring her words carefully, "I do appreciate your sympathy. And I do want you to know that the darkest part is already behind me. I also know that the journey ahead of me won't be easy ... I still miss her so much, and I don't know when or how that's going to go away ... I almost feel like I'm floating in a time warp, like in a dream, where I just keep floating, and every time I see something I think I want to grab onto, it disappears. Does that make any sense?"

Cathy laughed. "No, of course it doesn't," she said as her laugh turned to sobs. "I ... just ... miss ... her ... so ... much ..."

Cathy exhaled the last of her sobs, and began talking again. "I have lived too long trapped in this ghost, in the shell of the person I used to be. I'm not sure what person I will become, but she will take shape in time, somewhere, somehow. I have nothing but time now. And please, Mrs. Spellmeyer, allow me to thank you. Thank you for all you've done for Mallory's family. And thank you for your kind words."

Chapter 22

March 1984

*"You are human and fallible," wrote Charlotte Bronte in
Jane Eyre. It was part of a conversation questioning the possibility of full redemption, or at least, the likelihood of a mere
mortal resolving to be better and never wavering from that
resolve.*

*It is a fair statement. We are all human and fallible. We
may leap forward hopefully and then, reverting to our old,
imperfect selves, slide backward an equal distance.*

*But does it have to be that way? It is possible that an exam-
ined life full of love and service and humility can bring us, if
not to reclamation, at least to a better place than where we were?*

*I know only that from this day forward, every positive thing
I do, every human being I help, and maybe, one day, every word
I write that touches the heart of a complete stranger, will be done
in your honor, in your name, in your everlasting grace.*

May 1984

Although George Dickleman had been annoyed that one

of his first-year teachers was moonlighting as a detective trying to solve a missing-persons case that hit too close to home, George was secretly pleased that Sam Field, through his contacts at Ethel Walker, had been able to help deflect the crime to the other campus. George offered, and Sam accepted, a contract from Avon Old Farms to teach again in the 1984-85 school year.

At the insistence of underclassmen JV soccer players who were moving up to varsity, and after a formal invitation from varsity head coach Juan Ortega, Sam accepted the position of assistant varsity coach. "Maybe we're robbing from JV to have it this way," Juan laughed to Sam, "but I think the two of us together might just prove formidable."

"Can Reese move up with us?" asked Sam.

Juan looked at Sam and smiled. "Sure," he said. "And then maybe I'll figure out why you have such affection for that plump little wiseass. Okay, no, not really. I get a kick out of him too."

***

Mario Arpante phoned Jackie Spellmeyer to thank her once again for solving the Mallory Harding case and clearing his son Tomas' name.

"I told you, he's a good kid," Mario said. "And I know he would never do anything to harm a woman."

"How is he doing at UConn?" she asked. "Did he have a good baseball season?"

"Very good," Mario said. "He hit three-fifteen."

Jackie wasn't sure what that meant exactly, though she was vaguely aware that it was some sort of percentage. What she did know was that anything over .300 was pretty good—especially after hearing Jerry complain that the Red Sox weren't winning in spite of Wade Boggs and Jim Rice both hitting over .300.

"Oh," added Mario, "he's been recruited to play summer ball in the Cape Cod League. Brewster Whitecaps.

"Well," Jackie replied, "We usually take a week on the Cape in August. We'll have to come watch him some night!"

"Let me know when—I'll leave tickets for you!" said Mario.
***

Sam, Kevin Doolan, Steve Morrow, and several other teachers went to O'Laughlin's for one last pub night before summer break.

Sidling up to the bar to order his second pint, Sam said to the bartender, "Look, Kieran, I gotta ask you. Are you really Irish?"

"No," Kieran replied with a sigh, winking across the room to Kevin and Steve. "I'm actually from Iowa."

Sam wheeled around to face his table "See! He exclaimed triumphantly, but the others, and Kieran, just broke into laughter. "Laddie," Kieran exclaimed, his brogue rising to new sing-songy heights, "I don't know the source of your delusion about this, but I'm the real deal. County Clare. I can show you my passport if you like. Ancestors came over during the Great Potato Famine of the 1880s."

On his way back to the table, it occurred to Sam that the famine was actually in the 1840s—and that unless has family had gone back to live for a time in Ireland, Kieran couldn't very well claim to be from County Clare. But he decided to leave it alone. "Probably just another deliberate trap to embarrass me," he thought to himself.

***

"That's very good, Vanessa. I like how you have described this scene so far. I almost feel like I'm in the room."

"Really?"

Cathy St. John smiled at the girl seated across from her at a wooden table. "Now tell me, what were you feeling during your father's visit?"

Vanessa looked up at Cathy with big brown eyes as she considered the question. "Angry. Angry at first. Mad at him for not being there. But then I looked at him, and I just felt sad."

"Go on. Anything else?"

Vanessa wiped a tear from her eye, composed herself, and began talking. "I realized how much I missed him. And how I couldn't wait for these six months to be over. And then he promised to take care of me and make sure I stayed away from the wrong people."

"And how was he feeling?"

"Sad," she replied. "Sad, but also kind and loving. And I felt like he really regretted that he wasn't around when it all happened."

"How could you tell?"

"By the things he said. And also ..."

"What?" asked Cathy.

"The way he covered his eyes with his hands when he started crying. And then he rubbed them really hard. And the way he looked at me and smiled and said how much he loved me and how happy he is that I'm OK."

All right," said Cathy. "Let's make this story even better. Describe everything you just told me about the way he broke down crying and then rubbed the tears away. Make it visual, like a movie. And don't be afraid to quote what he said. Bring him to life. I bet you can make the reader cry too."

"Do you think you can do that?" asked Cathy, "I mean, write some more emotion into the story with visuals?"

Vanessa looked up at Cathy and smiled, even as she fought back tears. "Yes, I think I can do that," she said.

"I didn't even think I could write," Vanessa said. "Thank you so much."

Cathy enjoyed coaching the other girls' writing; a few of them were also meeting with her once a week for poetry appreciation. The St. John family attorney had negotiated nine months in a residence for female teenage offenders, followed by probation and community service. Cathy had resolved from the outset to make the best of it.

One day in June, a letter arrived addressed to Catherine St. John. The return address was in Summit, New Jersey. She opened it slowly, then began reading.

Cathy,

>After giving it much thought, I decided to reach out to you. This is from me only, as my wife approaches her grief differently than I do. I believe in the idea of forgiveness, and I also believe that at heart you are a good person who loved Mallory very much,

even if it went too far. I know in my own heart that you did not seek this outcome.

We can never have Mallory back; we can only have the memories.

But you are still here, with the promise of a full life ahead of you. In the name of forgiveness and the heavenly light I feel from my daughter, I wish you the best in your future. I'm sure you will carry a heavy heart for years to come; I sincerely hope you will find a path to overcome that. I hear you are an outstanding writer. Perhaps that will play some part in your future endeavors.

Don't be afraid to reach out to me at whatever point down the road it feels right to do so.

Sincerely,
Charles Harding

A staff member saw the tears streaming down Cathy's face and asked if she was okay.

"Yes, I'm okay," she replied.

"I think you're doing great work with the other girls," the staffer added.

"Oh, thank you," Cathy smiled. "That means a lot to me. More than you know."

***

George Dickelman strolled through the Avon campus the day before graduation, talking to a 14-year-old boy about Avon campus life, academic opportunities, and the school's many sports programs. "I hear you're a pretty good hockey player," George said, smiling. Next to him, the boy's svelte and sophisticated mother, decked out in a stylish print sundress, smiled back at George.

The mother, discreetly falling back a couple of steps and then stepping forward again on George's side, asked him, in a hushed tone, "You have the number I left you, right?"

George just smiled and patted his shirt pocket.

***

After graduation, Sam and the other faculty circulated among the seniors to wish them well. The underclassmen were still on campus, and at one point, Sam saw Reese Gilmartin approaching him.

"Did Juan ask you to be equipment manager for varsity?" Sam asked.

"Yeah, I guess I'll do it, but does that mean I have to watch my mouth?" asked Reese.

"Well, maybe it just means you'll have to be more careful about picking your spots," Sam replied.

"Careful?" Reese asked with mock confusion. "Do I know that word? Do you have a dictionary on you?"

***

Sam folded laundry in preparation for packing his things and heading home to Northampton. He had been given the same apartment for the next school year, which made it more of his actual residence than just a temporary dorm room. That meant he could leave whatever belongings he wished, and, notwithstanding that he planned to spend most of the summer at his parents' house in Northampton, he could have access to the apartment anytime he wanted. Most older teachers stuck around because the school was their primary residence; and others took a summer course or two at Wesleyan, where Avon subsidized tuition for studies that led to advanced degrees in the disciplines they were teaching at the school.

As Sam mulled over which clothes and other items to take and which to leave, his mind drifted into a reverie about the joys and losses of the previous year. He felt particularly sorrowful about the death of Hank Shahinian, with whom he had formed a special bond as he began to understand the needs of the quiet, sometimes melancholy boy struggling to fit in at Avon. And he tried to check his anger and frustration with Hank's mother by telling himself—not quite convincingly—that parents had a right to raise their children as they see fit.

And then there was Mallory Harding—the girl he never met, but whose spirit seemed to call to him from the posters. Sam's eyes moistened as he thought of her, wondering if somehow, somewhere, she knew he had helped solve the case.

Finally, he thought of Maggie Duchesne. Forbidden love that was no longer forbidden. Except the cruel irony was that graduation also meant she was leaving his orbit for a new life far away in Washington, DC. His heart ached to think that after the emotional roller-coaster ride of their relationship during the school year, just like that, he might never see her again.

***

The day after Walker's graduation, Maggie drove to Avon in the new car she had received as a graduation gift from her parents. Warren, Annie and Maggie piled out, and walked over to knock on Sam's door.

"Hey, Mr. Field," Warren said, "Remember that day Annie and I walked away and left you alone with Maggie?"

"No more jailbait," said Annie. "She's a fully grown woman now. 18 going on 28." Annie giggled, and once again, they walked away.

Sam and Maggie looked at each other and burst into laughter. And gave each other a big hug. "Would you like to come in?" asked Sam.

"Well, who's the forward one now?" replied Maggie. "I can't stay long—I'm driving them up to New Hampshire. I'll come in for a minute or two."

They chatted about summer plans. Sam was going home again and painting houses. Katie had invited him to visit her for a few days in Boston; he didn't mention this. Maggie and several other Walker's girls were renting a house on Martha's Vineyard for a graduation trip in late June, then Maggie would go back to work at Christie's for about six weeks before heading to Georgetown in late August.

Maggie stood up and walked over toward Sam's phone, where there was a pad and pen for messages. "Who's Katie with the Boston area code?" she asked.

Damn, thought Sam. "Nobody important," he said, smiling sheepishly.

"She's your ex-girlfriend who isn't really quite 'ex' yet. Annie told me. And she came up in our conversation once before."

"We're still in touch."

Maggie looked at Sam and smiled.

"Well, you should be in touch. I don't know why I'm saying this, but I have a feeling she's good for you. Probably better for you than I am!"

"Now, we don't have to compare—"

Before Sam could finish, Maggie blurted out a confession. "If you don't already know this, Sam Field, yes, I was crazy about you ever since the day we met, and I was jealous of Katie. But hey, who am I to be jealous? You saw me kissing that boy in the doorway at Walker's that night, right? I know you did. I saw you. I think it freaked us both out."

"In any case," Maggie continued, "here's my number in New York. Feel free to write down your Northampton number for me. As much as I'd like to stay longer, I can't. I don't know when or how, but maybe we could see each other sometime."

"I think I'd like that," Sam said.

"In the meantime," Maggie said, "don't I get a kiss good-bye? Make that a guilt-free kiss goodbye!"

Sam walked over to her and put his arms around her waist. As their faces drew closer, Sam spoke.

"You know, I wonder, now that we can't get in trouble for this, maybe it won't be quite the same thrill."

"Speak for yourself," she said, pressing her lips into his slowly, then circling around them for an added tease. Finally, she dove in full force, with an element of lust he was sure she had not shown him before. And for the icing on the cake, she pulled away and began softly kissing his neck. As she returned her lips to his, she whispered, "I hope you're getting at least a little thrill out of this."

His breathing told him all she needed to know. That, and the way he slipped one hand off her waist and into his pocket.

"Oh dear, I hope I'm not making you uncomfortable," she said.

As Maggie noticed Sam fumbling with his erection, she had a sudden inspiration. She shot him an impish glance, grabbed the hand that was still on her waist, and thrust it up under her shirt until it rested firmly over her right breast. Sam gasped.

"You like that?" she said, laughing.

"Well ... Jeez ... Of course I do. Can't you tell?"

Maggie placed her free hand on the small of Sam's back and pulled him closer.

"Oh, yeah, I see what you mean!"

Then she burst out laughing.

"What's the matter?" Sam asked. "Is this not so much of a thrill for you?"

"Oh, I like it," Maggie replied. "And you know, Mallory used to say that sex should be fun and not to let anyone tell you otherwise." She laughed another hearty laugh.

"Which is why I thought about Miss Lavelle and what she'd think. But never mind—"

"*Miss Lavelle?*"

"She was this batty woman who tried to teach us how to repel horny boys, and practically fainted when one of the girls nonchalantly mentioned boys going up your shirt for a boob squeeze."

"Holy shit! I met her! I know exactly who you're talking about! She was drunk in a bar one night, making rude and ill-informed remarks about Mallory. But—story for another time."

"Well never mind her—and she's quite the mood killer, I can see that. But I have to get going anyway."

"You know what I realized from doing this without the guilt?" Maggie said. "All the other things that I'm free to think about, that crossed my mind while we were kissing. If you know what I mean."

Sam just sighed heavily, looked Maggie in her eyes, and shook his head slowly back and forth. "I still don't know what I'm going to do with you," he sighed.

"Oh, there they are, outside your door," she said. "I told them what time to come back. Annie asked me if I did that because I didn't trust myself. Smart girl. And she knows everything about me."

At the door, they kissed softly for another minute, and then Sam just held her, rubbing her back like he had done the first time they embraced back in the fall, when she had gotten upset and fallen into his arms.

"I will miss you," he said. "In fact, I think I'm going to miss you a whole lot."

"Me too." And with that, Maggie turned abruptly, walked out the door, met her friends, and drove away, a grown woman, no longer a silly prep-school girl.

www.ingramcontent.com/pod-product-compliance
Lightning Source LLC
Chambersburg PA
CBHW071600150726

48000CB00004B/1545